THE
VALENTINE'S
Hate

THE
VALENTINE'S

Hate

A Novel

SIDNEY HALSTON

AVON

An Imprint of HarperCollinsPublishers

HarperCollins books may be purchased for educational, business, or sales promotional use. For information, please email the Special Markets Department at SPsales@harpercollins.com.

FIRST EDITION

Designed by Diahann Sturge

Broken heart illustration © binik / Shutterstock

Library of Congress Cataloging-in-Publication
Data has been applied for.

ISBN 978-0-06-328639-9

22 23 24 25 26 LBC 5 4 3 2 1

For all the hopeless romantics.
You never know when Cupid will strike.

THE
VALENTINE'S
Hate

Prologue

Second Grade

"Oh honey, qué bella está," Lizzie's mom said as she adjusted the big red bow on Lizzie's headband.

"Where are my cards, Mami?"

Lorena reached for a plastic Walmart bag filled with Valentine cards that she'd spent all weekend filling out for the entire class. Lizzie had been so excited, sifting through each card and assigning them the names of each of her classmates based on what the card said or what animal was on the front. She'd saved a special one for Mariana, her best friend since kindergarten. It had a unicorn and said, "You're a magical friend."

There were a few mean kids in her class, like Roly Polinski and Karen Da Silva. Lizzie did not want to give them any cards or candy, but her mother had said, as she often did,

"Maybe your one act of kindness is what someone needs to turn their entire day around."

So, she'd given them a card. It wasn't the cutest card, but it was a card, nonetheless.

Aside from Halloween, Valentine's Day was the best day at school. They'd exchange cards and candies and she'd come home with a bag full of goodies, luxuries she didn't often have at home, no matter how many jobs her mom worked.

The yellow bus rounded the corner and honked; Lizzie practically vibrated with excitement.

"Have fun, mija."

"Bye, Mami," Lizzie yelled and waved as she jogged to the bus, her book bag bouncing up and down with each step. Just as she was about to reach the step to the bus, she was cut off by a boy. *Where'd he come from?* "Hey, watch it," she said, teetering on the edge of the sidewalk.

"Sorry," the boy murmured as he climbed up the steps, Lizzie behind him.

Lizzie had been living in the same house since she was two years old, after she and her family fled Cuba. She knew everyone from her block. Mr. and Mrs. Anderson, her neighbors on her right side, didn't have kids, they were old. Like sixty-years-old old. Ms. Baker, the neighbor on the left, had children who lived in Vermont. Needless to say, seeing a kid pop out of nowhere was very strange.

Shrugging it off, Lizzie climbed into the bus, smiling her customary greeting to the driver. Unfortunately, her smile was short-lived. Lizzie always sat in the same seat, but this new kid—the one who had almost caused her to fall down a minute ago—was there. "Hey, that's Lizzie's seat," Mariana scoffed.

"Says who?" the boy responded. He then opened a comic book and began to read, ignoring the two clearly upset girls.

Lizzie and Mariana both glared at the kid but since he didn't react, Lizzie was left with no other choice but to sit somewhere else. She stared at the boy, though. He looked strange. All the boys in her class had short dark hair and this boy had longish blond hair that fell forward and covered one of his blue eyes. She'd never really studied anyone with blue eyes before.

And she was annoyed. So darn annoyed. She had so much to tell her best friend. Over the weekend she'd seen two movies and her abuela had made her a new dress and she wanted to tell Mariana all about it. But this new boy was in the way. At least today would be fun and there'd be candy.

"Everyone, please give a warm welcome to Brian Anderson. He's new in class and comes here all the way from Boston." That was the first thing Mr. Rodriguez said after the morning announcements. Brian looked up from his book just long enough to give an awkward wave, blond hair covering his eyes. "Can anyone tell me where Boston is on the map?" When no one raised their hand, Mr. Rodriguez called on Brian, who shrugged and looked away.

How rude, Lizzie thought. Eventually, the attention shifted, and it was back to business as usual in class.

"That kid is weird," Ryan, another boy from Lizzie's class, said during lunch. "Super weird," someone else replied. Lizzie looked across the cafeteria table to see that Brian was sitting all alone in a corner, reading a comic book. He looked sad and she remembered all the stories her mom and abuela had told her about coming to this country and not knowing anyone.

"I don't think he's weird," Lizzie said to the group, even though she did. "He's just new and he doesn't know anyone. We should make him a card for the Valentine's Day exchange."

"And we can share our candies," Mariana suggested. Some of her friends agreed. Maybe Brian just needed to feel welcomed.

During recess, when they'd put away all their books and begun the valentine exchange, Lizzie gave out the cards to her girlfriends first. When she noticed Brian had not moved from his seat and was reading his comic book, she decided it was time to be the bigger person and introduce herself. "Hi. My name is Lisette, or Lizzie, actually. I made you a card and here are some M&M's; do you like chocolate?"

Brian looked up from his comic book without even a hint of a smile. "I hate chocolate," he said, took her card, and ripped it.

Stunned at what had just occurred, Lizzie felt her eyes begin to water. "I'm telling," she said.

"I don't care. Be a tattletale. Your card is stupid. Valentine's Day is stupid."

Eighth Grade

Are you sure this looks okay? I feel silly," Lizzie asked Mariana while looking at herself in the mirror. She wasn't used to seeing herself in a pink frilly dress.

"You look awesome, Lizzie," Mariana replied with a big smile on her freshly glossed pink lips. "How about me?" she asked while twirling so that her baby-blue dress poofed out like waves.

Lizzie rolled her eyes. Mariana knew she looked great. She was the most popular girl in class now and it wasn't only because she had long black hair that cascaded down her back, or perfect skin when everyone else seemed to have acne. It was also because she had boobs. At thirteen, Mariana was wearing a real bra and all the boys had noticed. The girls too. Yes, she was also supersmart and aside from Lizzie had the best grades in their class. But mostly, Lizzie felt it was the boobs that were causing Mariana this newfound popularity and self-confidence. "You look fantastic, as always," Lizzie said, while stuffing some toilet paper into her bra.

"Don't do that," Mariana said with a giggle and tried to stop her, but Lizzie sidestepped her and continued to stuff her bra until it couldn't take one more ply. "Aren't you excited, Lizzie? I can't believe it's our first school dance! I think Jimmy is going to ask me to dance. What do you think?"

"Totally," Lizzie replied. She wondered if anyone would ask her to dance. It was, after all, the Valentine's Day Dance and the first real school dance she'd attended.

"Qué lindas!" Lizzie's mother squealed as she walked into the room to find them all dressed up—glittered eyelids, flowy dresses, kitten-heeled shoes.

"Gracias," Mariana said.

"I offered to let Brian ride with us and pick him up on the way back," Lizzie's mom said. "He's waiting outside."

"No, Mom! Whyyyy?" Lizzie whined, joined by Mariana.

"Don't be mean, girls. You know Mr. and Mrs. Anderson don't drive. Poor Brian wouldn't have been able to go."

"Who cares," Lizzie said.

"Lisette Alonso. I don't like that."

"Sorry, Mom," Lizzie replied, feeling embarrassed.

"Remember one act of kindness may change someone's entire day."

When she stepped out of the house, Brian was waiting on the front porch, looking down, his hands in his pockets. He had on jeans and a white button shirt that was untucked and Converse sneakers. His grandmother had made him cut his hair short and it was at that awkward stage where it needed to be trimmed. "Hi, Brian," her mother said.

"Hello, Mrs. Alonso," he said in that now-deepish voice. Lizzie had noticed that a lot of the boys in her school now had deeper voices. In fact, she had noticed a lot of changes lately. Most girls now had breasts and curves and spent most of their free time talking about boys. Meanwhile, the boys were either ogling the girls or talking about having to shave their mustaches, which were really a barely noticeable fuzz growing over their lips that looked more like chocolate milk than hair. All these changes annoyed Lizzie, mostly because she wasn't changing. Not. At. All.

"You look very handsome, Brian," her mother said, and Lizzie and Mariana pretended to gag behind Lizzie's mother. Brian noticed and gave them the finger.

The trip to the dance was quiet and when they arrived, Brian went one way and the girls another. He had his own group of friends now. They were the weird kids who wore black clothes and eyeliner and were always talking about the newest superhero movies or sci-fi books.

Lizzie did notice that Karen Da Silva, a girl from their class, had started flirting with Brian this school year, and for some reason, Lizzie didn't like it. Maybe it was because Karen had never been particularly nice to Lizzie or maybe it was because Karen was always trying to get Brian's undivided attention. Brian wasn't cool or cute, he was mean, and when he wasn't ignoring her, he always had something rude to say. Lizzie didn't understand how everyone didn't see it.

As soon as she saw him walk in, Karen beelined straight toward his group of friends and handed him a little bag full of candied hearts. "Pick one, Bri. Tell me what it says."

Brian pulled one out and read, "Be mine."

Lizzie would bet anything that all of the stupid hearts said "Be mine."

"Of course I will, Bri."

Lizzie almost gagged. "What are you looking at?" Karen said when she caught Lizzie examining the way Karen's dress inched up way past the knee and the way she leaned in and laughed obnoxiously loud at whatever Brian was saying.

Lizzie didn't reply, she just looked away, hoping that no one could see her red cheeks. But of course, Karen didn't let it go. "Everyone knows she likes you, Brian. So sad," she said with a high-pitched laugh.

Lizzie whipped around and stomped toward them. "That is not true!" Mariana tried to stop her, but Lizzie could not, would not be stopped. "You're just a mean girl who doesn't know what else to say to get his attention. You have to put me down in—"

As Lizzie became emboldened in her diatribe, standing up for the bullied kids of the world, Karen slowly walked toward her. That was not how it happened in movies. Karen should have been so shocked by the words coming out of Lizzie's mouth that she'd cry and run away or apologize— but the bullies never approached like Karen was doing: slowly, predatorily. Lizzie stood her ground and didn't step away even though she felt like running.

All eyes were now on them.

Then Karen lifted her hand and just as Lizzie was about to block the slap across her face, Karen's hand went lower. Lizzie watched in horror as Karen pulled and pulled and pulled some more. It took a few jolting moments but then all the toilet paper from one of Lizzie's bra cups was now hanging down, lifelessly, from Karen's hand.

The entire school was now in hysterics, but no one more than Karen. "Aw . . . look, Bri, toilet paper titties." Then the rest of the class started chanting, "Toilet titties. Toilet titties."

The last thing Lizzie remembered before she ran home, literally all the way home, in tears was the look of shock on Brian's face.

Eleventh Grade

Lizzie was running late to school that day. Her mother hadn't been feeling great and she'd missed the bus. She ran to the office and got a tardy slip and then rushed to her locker to get her books. She ran past all the balloons and red hearts decorating the school halls. Until last year she hated Valentine's Day, but this year was different. She was dating Liam, her first boyfriend, and they had plans to go to the movies tonight. She had spent all evening baking him his favorite red velvet cupcakes and was holding them in one hand. The bell rang and students started to leave first period and spill out into the halls.

Rushing to open her locker, Lizzie screamed bloody murder when four lizards scurried out and onto her, the tray of cupcakes falling to the floor as she hopped up and down to get them off her.

Behind her, she heard a familiar laugh. "Happy V-Day, Lizard." Brian had started calling her Lizard, a play on Lizzie, a few years ago when he had found out she was scared of lizards one evening when she ran out of her house shrieking because she'd seen one inside. Brian and his grandfather had gone over and helped her mother remove the vermin from the house so that Lizzie would go back inside. Lizzie had stayed with Mrs. Anderson eating freshly baked cookies with milk while they waited. Eventually, Brian had held up the lizard by its tail and almost shoved it in her face before tossing it into his front yard. "You're safe now, the big bad lizard's been caught," he'd said.

"Thank you so much," she'd replied, sincerely grateful, but the jerk glared at her.

"Thanks a lot, Lizard; because of you, I missed the season finale of *Smallville*."

She'd tried to apologize but he'd slammed the door shut. That had been almost five years ago. But now, he'd gone too far, stuffing lizards into her locker.

Normally, Lizzie was even-tempered, but when it came

to Brian, she lost all sense of reason. She'd had enough. Enough with being picked on, enough with having to see Brian at every corner, enough of trying to be nice to the world's biggest jerk! Without much thought, Lizzie bent down and picked up a handful of mushed cupcakes and in a moment of fury threw it right in Brian's face with a triumphant grunt. He wasn't laughing anymore. At least now he had a reason to hate her. Before this moment, she hadn't done anything to deserve being the butt of his pranks or jokes. He stood there slack-jawed as clumped-up frosting fell from his face to the floor. Clearly, he hadn't expected her to retaliate. She felt exhilarated at having done it.

Unfortunately, the school security guard walked by at that moment, and they were both sent home for the rest of the day and suspended the day after that. Consequently, her mother grounded her and she couldn't go out with Liam that night and instead spent Valentine's Day in her room crying. For the umpteenth time, Brian Anderson had ruined Valentine's Day.

Chapter One

Lizzie

"The last thing I need is to be in Cancún during this merger, William," Lizzie whined into her cell phone as she waited for everyone to finish boarding the flight.

"I agree," William, her executive assistant, said. "But it's Mariana and you have to go."

With a long sigh she tried to relax. She'd given William very specific orders, three months ago when the wedding invitation arrived, to make sure she got on the plane and went to the wedding no matter what was happening with work. It had been almost a year since she'd last seen Mari and there was no way she could miss her best friend's special day. They still spoke or FaceTimed every day, but they had not physically been in the same room for far too long. Even during the last few years, their visits had been too short and too spaced out. An occasional Christmas or New Year's, a week during summer, or a quick trip abroad for a birthday bash. It was difficult to make time to fly to Miami when both of their schedules were so busy. Time seemed to move forward and before either of them knew, another month had passed by and plans hadn't been set. But, even if they hadn't been physically together as much as Lizzie would have liked, Mariana had remained the constant in Lizzie's life, and she'd do anything for her—even celebrate Valentine's Day.

"Pft . . . and on this weekend of all weekends. Who plans a wedding on Valentine's Day? So fuckin' cheesy, right?"

"Actually, it's not," William said. "It's kind of like the perfect day to get married. Valentine's on a Saturday. It's . . . ahhh . . . perfection," he sighed into the phone and Lizzie could picture his swoony expression. William was a romantic, through and through.

Lizzie almost gagged. "If I didn't love you so much, I'd fire you."

He laughed. "When you return, I'll take you out for our customary love-day-bashing pub crawl."

"Promise?"

"Promise."

"Fine. Fine. Anyway, remember to send me daily—no, hourly—updates on the merger."

"Yes, boss. Safe travels. I'm hanging up now."

She couldn't help but smile. Finding William was one of the best things that had happened to her in the last few years. She'd found herself homesick and lonely at her new job in London, and then William had strutted into her office for an interview after she'd posted an ad for an assistant. He wore a light pink linen suit, the pants ending right over the ankle, and he'd paired it with moccasin-like sockless shoes. It was a ridiculous style, yet it reminded her so much of Miami that she hired him on the spot. Anyone fierce enough to pull off *Miami Vice* was her kind of person. They became instant friends. After losing her mother five years earlier, and her grandmother the summer after high school, having friends like Mariana and William was what got her through the tough times.

The first leg of the trip, from London to Atlanta, was almost ten hours, so, being the terrible flyer that she was, she popped an Advil PM and prayed that the next time she woke up she'd be touching ground in the States to catch her connecting flight to Cancún, Mexico.

Brian

I'm supposed to have a window seat," Brian said to the flight attendant as he pulled up the e-ticket on his phone.

"That's your return flight, sir. See, it says February 15 right there. Today is February 10." Then, she turned and smiled one of those perfectly fake and perfectly practiced smiles. Brian knew better than to mess with that kind of gritted-tooth smile. He knew these types of women. They smiled and made the receiver feel warm and fuzzy, but in reality, she was thinking, *If you don't sit your ass down, I'll call the U.S. Marshals to escort you out.*

"Excuse me. Pardon. Sorry." Brian looked up as a woman in sunglasses, a scarf, a turtleneck, and unruly hair shuffled her way down the row making a big ruckus. "I'm so sorry. My connecting flight was delayed and . . . anyway." She showed the attendant her ticket and Fake Smile pointed toward Brian. His hope of having an empty seat between the ginormous bodybuilder and his aisle seat was crushed. *Here the comes middle seat.*

Pushing her glasses down her nose, she looked his way. For a second, she seemed slightly familiar but then all her chaotic energy overtook any previous thoughts he had and they turned to annoyance. The woman must've said "pardon" and "excuse me" a dozen times as she pushed her carry-on down the aisle and then stopped and lifted it up to the overhead bin.

When she was finished, she exhaled and a chestnut-brown piece of hair that had fallen from behind her ear flew up and then landed back over her sunglasses-covered eye.

"I think that's my seat," she said, pointing to the middle seat. There was plenty of room for her to scooch through, but Brian could already tell that if he didn't get his ass up and allow her through, this was going to turn into a spat.

Without having to have a single conversation with the woman, he could tell she was an introverted man's worst nightmare. So, he got up and let her pass.

"Thanks," she said as she moved through, hitting the people in front of them with her purse. "Oh, sorry. Sorry."

"Maybe if you take off your sunglasses, you'd be able to see where you're going," Brian said under his breath. Instantly regretting it. Engaging in a conversation was not in his plans.

She stopped and pushed the glasses down again. This time their eyes met. He knew those eyes. It had been a long time, but those eyes were not friendly eyes. *Oh shit*. Yet, his belly did a strange loop the loop at seeing her again after all these years.

Since she didn't seem to recognize him, Brian decided best not to say anything. After all, the woman hated him, and he hated her. Unfortunately, they were close and awkwardly positioned in the small confines of the cabin, and the surly stewardess had once again announced that the overhead bins needed to be closed and that everyone needed to take their seats. "My contact lenses fell out and my spare are in my luggage; these have prescription lenses. Without them, I won't be able to see a thing. It's not like I want to wear sunglasses inside." Unlike the flight attendant, there was no fakeness in her tone. She was undoubtedly unhappy.

With his hands held up in defense, he said, "No need to explain. Let me help you with this." As he tried to reach for her bag, she held on to it tighter. Yep, some things never changed. She was just as combative now as she was back then.

"I'm fine, I'll put this under my seat," she said with a shrug, so Brian let it go, closed the overhead bin, and plopped down onto his own seat. Yep, that was definitely Lisette Alonso. Lizzie, his neighbor and childhood nemesis. Pain in the ass of his formative years. The girl did not like him from the day they first met, and that had seemingly continued well into their thirties, by her glare and body language. It was as if her DNA were programmed to hate him on sight. She didn't even recognize him, and she was oozing vitriol. Brian had to hold in a smirk when he caught her looking at Bodybuilder Dude's body spilling over into her seat.

Ain't karma a bitch?
This was going to be a long-ass flight.

Lizzie

Lizzie was exhausted. But, by the commotion around her and the various announcements in both English and Spanish, it seemed that they had landed. *Oh! Oh no!* She was resting her head on the person sitting next to her. *Oh God!* The embarrassment of it all. Her flight had been long, and the Advil PM had left her drowsy and loopy. The sunglasses didn't help make things better. She righted her head and wiped her chin. Yep—drool. *Excellent job, Lizzie.*

She pulled off her sunglasses and wiped her eyes. "I'm sorry. I'm so embarr—" She began to apologize to her neighbor, when she got a good look. Not just a good look, she did a double take and squinted. "Is that . . . are you . . . Brian? Brian Anderson?"

"Yep," he said with a shit-eating grin. The fact that she'd rested her head on someone she knew should have made her feel less embarrassed, but the shoulder belonged to Brian the boy next door, who'd made her life miserable whenever he could. The bane of her existence. She'd rather have rested her head on the propellers of the plane than on Brian Freakin' Anderson's shoulder.

She wiped the cobwebs out of her eyes and tried to get the confusion out of her head. "Is this a nightmare? It has to be a nightmare."

"It was for me. My shirt is covered in drool and makeup," he said, looking down at his shoulder.

"What are you doing here? In Mexico? Were you invited to Mariana's wedding?" How could her best friend not have told her? Her heart was racing. No. It couldn't be.

"Who? What? No."

"'Who?' Oh, please, you know very well who Mariana is."

"Your friend? From school? That was a thousand years ago. Why would I be going to her wedding?"

"I don't know. Why else would you be going to Cancún?"

"Because of work. I'm working this weekend," he said and she was even more confused. The jet lag was setting in.

"What the hell kinda work takes you to Cancún?"

"A press tour."

Her brows furrowed. "A press tour? For what? Are you some kind of actor?"

"I wrote a book that is being made into a movie. Well, it's already made. It comes out this summer."

"You wrote a book?"

"Yes. Nine of them, actually. They're a series."

"Oh. Well . . . okay." What the hell else could she say? He was staring at her, as confused as she was. His eyes were bluer than she remembered, even through the black-rimmed glasses, and his hair was shorter. Where it used to be disheveled and longish, constantly falling over his eyes, now it was short on the sides and neatly combed to the side. He wasn't as pale or thin anymore, either. He was tan, like he hung out in the sun often, and from the little she could tell from the angle they were in, he had bulked up a bit. "After having to endure years of Sunday dinners with you, I have to admit I'm impressed. I didn't even know you knew how to read."

"You wouldn't have known if I read or not because you were always too busy yapping your mouth off. I always did wonder if your tongue got tired from all the talking. Or maybe a sore throat?"

"Pleasant as always, Anderson."

"You bring it out of me, Alonso. How my grandparents liked you so much is beyond me."

Her mother and grandmother had loved Brian and his family, and Sunday dinners were a constant for years. They'd alternate between the two homes. While the adults cooked and talked, Brian and Lizzie fought over the remote control or battled over a Nintendo game. It was the only time they'd really had conversations, if arguing over which game to play or what show to watch counted as conversation. She hated admitting that she was impressed. A book and a movie. Wow. She made a mental note to look him up later and check whether he was lying.

They both reached for their phones at the same time and tried to tune each other out.

"Please stay seated, there's a delay at the terminal," the overhead voice said.

Lizzie tossed her head back and closed her eyes. "Of course there is," she murmured.

"Bad flight?"

"I just want to get off this plane and get to my hotel. I have been in, on, or around a plane for more hours than I care to count."

"So I take it you don't live in Miami anymore?" he asked.

"Nope. I've been living in London for the last five years."

He turned his head toward her and his eyes were wide. "Well, that's definitely a bit further than Miami."

She chuckled. "You?"

"Boston," he said. She remembered that's where he lived before he moved in with his grandparents. She went back to her phone and so did he.

"Shit," he whispered, mostly to himself, but she turned her head to him. He was entranced with whatever he was reading on his phone. He moaned and groaned a few times and stopped typing then began again.

"Uhhh . . . everything okay?" she finally asked, when it became even weirder that she wasn't acknowledging all the noise he was making from his seat, one inch from hers.

"No," he said gruffly, but didn't explain.

"O . . . kay," she said just as snarky, but his phone rang at that same time.

With a groan, Brian answered. "Hello." He sounded like he was actually in pain. "You know I only agreed to this because you were coming. You know I can't. But— No. It's not that easy for me. I really don't think—Louise . . . this is going to be a fucking disaster. Yeah, fine. Okay, I hope you feel better."

He hung up.

"Girlfriend problems?" *Or maybe wife.*

"I wish."

He didn't elaborate and she didn't ask, but his leg was bopping up and down.

"Do you think you can stop that?" She placed her hand on his knee. "It's a little annoying."

"Sorry," he said absently. She opened her emails and started scrolling. William had copied her on everything and even though it sometimes felt as if the company would fall apart without her, everything was fine; there wasn't much William couldn't handle.

"It's just that Louise, my agent, was coming with me. We were meeting here, but she's sick and can't make it," he said as if they'd been mid-conversation.

"I hope she's okay."

"Me too. It's the flu, apparently. She says she'll live." Apparently, Louise had a sardonic sense of humor.

"Oh, well, that's good."

"No, it's not good. It's awful. Not that she'll live. I'm grateful about that, obviously. I can't do this thing alone. She was supposed to be here, that's the only reason I agreed to do it."

"Why? You're a big boy."

He let out a breath. "There's no way for me to say this without sounding like an arrogant douche but I'll preface it with saying, I didn't ask for it and I certainly don't want it . . ." He paused, and she noticed a pained look on his face.

"For God's sake, spit it out already."

"You know Violet Gram?"

"The movie star?"

He nodded. "She's the lead in the movie. During filming we got close. I gave her my thoughts as to how I saw the character in my head and we went to dinner a few times. I thought it was professional and platonic but turns out, she didn't want to just be friends."

"Are you saying the biggest, hottest movie star on the planet wants to sleep with you?"

He pinched the bridge of his nose instead of replying.

"I thought she was married." She snapped her fingers,

trying to recall the name. She liked Hollywood gossip just as much as the next guy but having been in Europe for the last few years, she hadn't been as focused on the latest hot topics. "Scott Barker, right?"

"Yep. That's her husband." He seemed truly miserable.

"I'm sorry I'm not finding sympathy in any of this."

"I don't want her in that way but she's a huge star and everyone keeps reminding me how lucky I am that she agreed to play the main role. I can't piss her off. There's still two more movies in the works and she's known for throwing temper tantrums when she doesn't get her way. If she drops out of the subsequent movies, that'll end my career. Or so I've been told. Repeatedly."

"Oh, poor you . . ."

He rolled his eyes.

"Maybe you misunderstood. Women can be friends with men. I'm sure you're misreading the situation."

"I'm not. Trust me."

Unable to help it, she put his name in the search bar on Google and nothing popped up. "What's the name of these famous books of yours?" she asked.

He hesitated before replying. "You think I'm lying, don't you?"

"For months you told me that your grandmother's shepherd's pie was made with a shepherd."

"You're the dumb one who believed it."

"I was eight years old and you gave me a big dissertation on how I was offending your Irish ancestors by not eating it."

"You were such an ass."

"You weren't a walk in the park either. Remember how
we tied for first place in the fifth-grade spelling bee and we
had to share the trophy but you broke it before it ever made
it to my house?"

"It was an accident!"

"Sure it was," she said. "Whatever. Are you going to tell
me the name of your books or what?"

"Invaders," he whispered.

Even she knew about the Invaders series. "That's what
you wrote?" She had to shake her head to make sure she
wasn't hearing things. The books and the trailers to the
movie were everywhere these days. He nodded, almost im-
perceptibly, and she typed "Invaders" into the search bar.

She gasped when the images began to load.

"No, no. Please don't," he begged but it was too late.

"You're in *People* magazine's 'Sexiest Man' edition?"

"Oh God," he said, looking genuinely mortified. "I told
you this is all new to me. I never asked for any of it."

"How did I not know this?"

"Because I write under a pen name and never do interviews," he said. "I have pretty major social anxiety. I can't
do this stupid meet-and-greet alone and I'll probably screw
up and piss Violet off and shit all over my career. The week
is going to be a disaster. Maybe I can get Greg to fly down.
He's great with speeches." He said it out loud but he was
typing and mostly talking to himself.

"Wait . . . what . . . I have so many questions." Now

she was not only fully awake, she was turned toward him, well, as much as she could in the tight confines of the seat.

"Social anxiety is a real thing. I swear. Google it."

"I know it's a thing, Anderson. That's not the part that is causing me to go into shock, it's the *People* magazine part and the book and the movie star . . . it's . . . No, that's . . . no. You're just, I don't know, Brian, the asshole who used to pull my hair and burp on demand. Who's Greg, by the way?"

"A lot has happened since grade school, Lizzie. And stop scrolling through that." He took the phone from her hand and flipped it over. "Greg's a friend. He's actually a musician so he's cool with large audiences. But he's not available," he said, reading his phone. "Damn it."

"Let's not gloss over the *People* magazine situation."

"I wasn't on the cover or anything. I was toward the back. A tiny little photo. 'Most eligible author' category. It's so embarrassing, I don't even want to talk about it anymore." He looked like he wanted to run out of the airplane just saying those words. Regardless, being in the magazine was a pretty major accolade, she knew. "Anyway, that's neither here nor there. I don't want to do this alone. I'll say the wrong thing and screw it up. I only agreed to this because the Latin American tour is smaller in scale than the American one and because Louise was going to be here as a buffer." He turned back to his phone and started frantically texting.

She shrugged. It was hard to feel any sympathy for someone who used to call her Lizard or someone whose current problem involved having too many people love him. The effects of the Advil PM and the jet lag, combined with having Brian half a foot from her face, caused a small giggle to escape her lips. "Am I dreaming? Is this a candid-camera situation?" she said, mostly to herself. She was fatigued, utterly incapable of thinking straight or processing all the information that she'd learned in the last ten minutes, which was why the solitary giggle turned into a full-blown fit of exhausted laughter a moment later. It wasn't that she wasn't sympathetic to his problem, it was that she just needed to get off the plane and into a bed so that she could go back to being a rational human being again.

Brian

Admitting all of this to the woman who once got him grounded for a month for pouring chocolate milk inside her book bag, when it was obviously Roly Polinski who'd done it, was mortifying. Lizzie looked both surprised and unimpressed as she took it all in. Brian hated to be the center of attention and he loathed talking about himself but she'd been right next to him when Louise called and he just ended up spitting it all out.

She opened her mouth to say something but then closed

it and burst out in laughter. She was laughing so hard, in fact, she woke up Bodybuilder Guy, who was still snoozing despite their landing and taxi to the gate. "Sorry. Sorry," she said, when he grunted at her and then closed his eyes again, and she turned her attention back to Brian. "This all sounds ridiculous, you know that, right?"

"I know!" His lip was slightly upturned, as if he was trying his best to hold in a smile. The only reason he wasn't offended that she was outright laughing at him was because he had thought it absurd so many times in the past. It was still unfathomable to him that he had women fawning over him. "Fawning" was actually a major understatement since he'd gotten underwear thrown at him, full nudes in his DMs, propositioned for three-ways, cosplay groupies begged him to sign his name on pretty much any surface of their body, and Violet Gram was actually trying to seduce him . . . It was more than any introverted man needed or wanted. Top it off with being the center of attention on a stage in a few days—he began to sweat at the thought.

"Oh shit, you're serious. You're actually freaking out about this," she said, no longer laughing.

"Unfortunately," he answered, swallowing the lump in the back of his throat.

"Admittedly unexpected," she said, unbuckling her seat-belt.

Unexpected that he was successful or unexpected that he had major social awkwardness? He was about to ask but people began to stand up around them. During his minor meltdown, he had failed to notice that they must've given everyone the okay to deplane.

"Well, I can't say it's been wonderful to see you again, but you did keep me entertained during the last few minutes and I did sleep on you . . . so, thanks," she said as she motioned for him to step aside. Bodybuilder Guy now also seemed impatient to get out of his seat. Brian moved over and let them out and then he reached for the overhead compartment. He took down the bag he saw her put up earlier, followed by his own bag. She gave an awkward thank-you. "Good luck. See you around, Anderson." She used the name she'd always called him. It was said with disdain, as if the last thing she'd ever want to do was "see him around." That's how it had always been with them—instant dislike. Like oil and water.

"Hopefully not, Alonso," he said, and she gave him an obligatory wave and walked toward the exit. Unfortunately, he stared at her as she walked away.

Damn, the scrawny little brunette had really filled into her body. She had always been pretty, even if a pain in the ass, but she was beautiful now.

In school he wanted to be invisible, but she always called him out on his shit and made him feel as if everyone were looking at him. The first day they'd met, he was doing everything he could not to cry. His parents had just died and the last thing he wanted was to giggle about cutesy cards and candies. Through the years, Miss Goody-Goody with her perfect grades and sweet disposition was the topic of conversation all the time. "She's such a nice girl," his granny would say. "She can probably tutor you in algebra," his grandfather would add, even though Brian had almost perfect grades. He was sick of her and her perfect little life. But enemies or not, he wasn't blind. She was always fresh-faced, even when other girls had started wearing makeup, because she didn't need it. Her tan skin was flawless, she had big brown expressive eyes, and two deep dimples at the corners of her pink full lips. In fact, she should have looked awkward with her all-too-big features: owl-like eyes, chipmunk-looking cheeks, and big goldfish lips. Somehow, though, it had worked. She was stunning.

Now, that tan skin seemed glossy, as if she'd just applied moisturizer, except he knew for a fact in the last three hours, all she'd done was drool and snore on his shoulder, not to mention leave a smudge of what looked like makeup. Truthfully, he hadn't noticed her falling asleep on him, because he had fallen asleep himself and only woken up when she'd startled awake.

Regardless, he didn't have a chance to think too much about Lizzie when his mind was filled with the horror that awaited him this weekend at the Villas de Amor.

Chapter Two

Brian

The closer the cab got to the Villas de Amor, the faster Brian's heart beat. This wasn't just a press junket. They'd booked him to do a signing and a meet-and-greet as part of the planned events. He didn't want any of the things that came with the industry. He just wanted to write. If he wasn't writing, he was in his garage at home, building furniture. He liked the peace that working with his hands brought him. He couldn't think of anything else when he was hyper-focused on describing the intricacies of the desolate valley full of overgrown weeds and wild and rabid wolves that used to be Manhattan, or creating the ornate details of the inlay of a coffee table. Anything that kept his hands and brain busy was what he craved.

He didn't want to be on Instagram, he certainly was

not the TikToking type, and he absolutely and unequivo-
cally did not want to stand in front of a huge audience and
talk. *What would he even say?* A book signing slash meet-
and-greet was about as extroverted as he could get. Plus,
Violet would be there, and she was pushy as hell. Getting
her to back off was going to be a huge challenge. First, she
was married, and second, she was one of the world's most
known actresses and was used to being the center of attention, something he avoided at all costs. Beautiful or not,
he was not at all interested in her. Luckily, the actor playing Zeth, Brad Kilpatrick, was in New Zealand filming a
series and would not be available for the tour. Brad was an
even bigger movie star than Violet and the number of fans
who would've been swarming the resort would have been
too much for Brian to handle. How they thrived in the
limelight was something Brian would never understand.

With a long sigh, he stepped out of the black Escalade
that had been waiting for him at the airport and into the
warm Mexican sun, regretting ever having come. The driver
took his bag out of the trunk and hotel security greeted
him. He took in a long inhale of the salty air reminiscent
of Miami. Maybe it was because he'd just seen Lizzie after
so many years, or maybe it was the warm ocean air, but he
was suddenly hit with a deep pang of nostalgia. Over the
years he had occasionally thought about Lizzie. She'd been
a pretty big part of his life back then, even if she hadn't
known it.

From kindergarten to high school, it was a reel of Lizzie

during the day, tormenting him with her constant good grades and shitload of friends, and the sadness of being home with his sweet but elderly grandparents in the afternoon.

Snap out of it, Brian.

It was time to put these stupid memories out of his mind and get on with it. He put on his Red Sox cap, plastered on a smile. Since he used a pen name and avoided interviews, not many people knew what he looked like. There were some fans who scoured the internet and found old photographs of him, or his headshot from the book, but his face wasn't as known as the actors' in his movie. Nevertheless, he braced himself for what possibly awaited him. Lines of photographers and groups of people holding books and movie posters loitered around the front entrance of the resort, but security flanked him and ushered him inside in a choreographed move that took him out of the melee and into the sanctuary of the hotel in less than a minute. Most of them were waiting for the movie stars and not for Brian, although he did hear his name called out as he walked briskly inside.

Brian went straight to the lobby to check in, noticing that the photogs and fans weren't allowed inside. He felt relief, a moment of respite before the long weekend ahead.

Plastered front and center against one of the enormous walls was a cover of his book with a Spanish title. It was easily ten feet tall, with his headshot on a corner. If he had any doubt that this weekend was going to be overwhelming, the huge poster with his big head staring back at him cemented it. The movie poster was on the other side, just as enormous. He groaned and turned toward reception.

Brian walked up to the lady at the front desk, whose name tag said *Patricia*. "Ah, Señor Anderson. Welcome! Look, it is you." She pointed to the poster behind him, as if he could have possibly missed it. "We are so excited to have you here. We have provided you with our best villa," she said with a big smile, handing him a keycard. She then put two fingers on her lips and blew out a shrill whistle that startled Brian. A short, bald man scurried over at her beck. "Pablo, this is Mr. Anderson."

"Ay, señor. It is such a pleasure to meet you."

Brian's brows furrowed but he stuck out his hand to greet the man, who took it very tightly and a bit overenthusiastically.

"Pablo will be your ambassador while you are here. Anything that you need, anything at all, he will make sure you have it."

"I don't think that will be necessary."

"Not necessary?" Pablo said, as he divested Brian of his luggage and started to roll it away. "It is not only necessary, Señor Anderson, it is a must. An honor, really. My son, Pablito, loves your books. We are big, big fans." Brian pushed his hat lower on his head and looked down as he walked to wherever Pablo was leading him.

This seemed to be the resort's main building, with an enormous lobby, walls towering up and up, as far as the eye could see. The lobby was buzzing with people, since it had a bar right smack in the middle of it.

They walked out to a tiki torch–lined covered walkway, as if they were headed to the pool, but instead they made a left. There was a grouping of independent suites, or villas, on the east side of the property.

"Here it is," Pablo said and unlocked the door. He held it open for Brian and then followed inside. "You like?"

Brian's jaw fell open. Growing up in the poorer part of Miami with his retired grandparents, who had a fixed income, and even with the luxuries he'd seen during the last few years as his books became hits, he still wasn't used to all of this wealth. "This is . . . wow."

Pablo put his luggage in a corner and then walked to the far end of the villa and opened the blinds, revealing a view of the ocean. "You have direct access to the beach. The master bedroom is there," he pointed to the right, "and there is a guest room here," he pointed to the left. "Your kitchen and dining room," he said. "The refrigerator is stocked but if there is anything you desire just let me know. Would you like for me to help you unpack?"

"No. No. This is amazing. I'm good, Pablo, thank you."

"After you settle in, perhaps you would like a drink. There is a private bar for villa guests right outside on the left. It is happy hour until seven."

"Thank you, Pablo." He could use a drink . . . or two.

Lizzie

After a day of flying, Lizzie was exhausted and all she wanted to do was go to bed.

"I am so sorry, miss. There has been an unfortunate incident and the rooms on the west wing have flooded, and we are overbooked due to various events in the area."

"What!" She wanted to scream and cry but mostly sleep.

"But it's no problem." The woman plastered on a theatrical smile. "We will be transporting all the guests to a nearby hotel until the problem is resolved. The accommodations are excellent and—"

"No. No no no." Did Mariana know about this? Lizzie had taken the precaution of flying in a day before the rest of the wedding party in order to get a good night's sleep and get over her jet lag, and now she was being moved.

"First of all, how far is this other hotel, and second, I'm supposed to be attending a wedding here in a few days: Is that still happening? Have the bride and groom been notified?"

"We have not informed the parties. It is not possible to call all the guests."

"It is possible," Lizzie argued. "My friend is getting married here and she should know if her wedding will be canceled!"

"The bridal suite is on the other side of the property, which is also where the reception takes place. They will not be affected. Some party guests, however, also have to be moved to the other hotel and we will inform them upon arrival."

"And the distance . . ."

"It is only a short forty-five-minute drive."

"Forty-five minutes! That is not short."

"Sixty, tops."

"There has to be something closer. There are so many hotels in this area, I saw them on the drive here."

"There's a big event happening this weekend and most hotels are booked. Keep your eyes open, you might see a few movie stars," the lady said excitedly.

Lizzie rolled her eyes. Of course . . . the big event was the press tour Brian had told her about. Brian and his stupid book were now ruining Mariana's wedding. Although it would be a small wedding, Marianna surely wanted all her guests to be in the same location so that they could spend time together without having to trek from one resort to another.

Lizzie could cry. But she didn't seem to have any choice in the matter. "Fine. How do I get there?"

"Well, the shuttle just left. It should be back in about ninety minutes."

Of course it had. Forty-five minutes one way and forty-five minutes back, then she had a forty-five-minute ride to the hotel. "Here are some vouchers for free drinks at the bar. Please help yourself."

Lizzie yanked them from her hands. "I will help myself, thank you very much."

"You are very welcome, miss," the woman said with a sincere smile. Lizzie's irritation was obviously lost in translation.

She dragged her luggage to the bar and ordered a vodka soda, not in the mood for a fruity cocktail, and then sat down to wait. She unlocked her phone and logged in to the hotel's Wi-Fi, which was sponsored by none other than the Invaders series.

Jeez.

Out of curiosity, she clicked on the link. There were almost a hundred authors attending the event, some familiar names included. She clicked on the link for "attending authors" and looked up Brian's name but it wasn't there. There was, however, a B. Anderson.

She knew who B. Anderson was because his books were everywhere these days. She wasn't much of a reader but she didn't live under a rock. She clicked on the link and the photo of B. Anderson loaded onto the screen. "Holy shit," she whispered. B. Anderson, the famous author of the Invader series, was Brian Anderson. He had really, really undersold himself earlier. She had been so surprised by the *People* magazine thing she hadn't continued snooping. It seemed like appearing in the magazine was the smallest of all his accomplishments.

The Invader series was huge. It was written for young adults but because of the forbidden love between some sort of alien and an angel or a vampire or something supernatural, it had become a sensation among women of all ages.

"I'm going to start thinking that you're stalking me."

Speaking of the devil.

She turned her head to see Brian walking her way. She quickly put her phone down, wondering if he'd seen her looking him up. "Oh shit, it's you!"

He furrowed his brows, misunderstanding her. How had she missed that earlier? She pointed to the wall behind him where there was a huge photo of him and his book. He looked over his shoulder and then pinched the bridge of his nose, just as he'd done on the plane. He'd changed into loose-fitting jeans and a white linen shirt that accentuated bulky biceps. He looked good. Annoyingly good.

She, on the other hand, must've looked like a hot mess, slouched over and defeated, on a pink velvet chaise in the middle of the lobby drinking vodka by herself.

"You're everywhere."

"Such a delight." He grinned and then sat next to her. "You look miserable."

She gave him the finger and said, "My room's flooded and I'm being relocated. I'm tired and cranky and not really up to whatever snarky remark you're going to throw at me."

"Says the woman that laughed at me for three straight minutes when I mentioned my career."

She rolled her eyes. That was about all the fight she had in her.

"I have—" he began but then waved his hand. "Never

mind." He stood and gave her a sad little shrug. "Good luck. Hopefully we won't have to see each other for another fifteen years."

That'll be too soon, she started to say but as soon as he turned, the most obnoxious and loud noise began from behind them. So loud, in fact, Lizzie jolted up to see what was happening. "What in the hell?"

"Oh shit. Oh no. No no no," Brian said.

"What is that?"

"Bringet and Volten," he whispered, as if she was supposed to know what the hell he was talking about.

"What?"

"From my novel. Supporting characters."

"Still not following."

"They're dressed as characters in my novels."

"How flattering. So why do you look like you're about to bolt?"

"They take it very seriously."

"Doesn't seem so bad. They're fans, suck it up, buttercup."

He glared at her. "I love my fans," he said as if correcting her. "I'm so flattered and grateful to see them. But they want me to be their Zeth. Some of them have millions of followers and they want to record all our interactions and then dissect them online."

"Zeth? What the fuck is that?"

"The hero in the book. They want me to role-play the romantic scenes. This is partly why I don't go to these things. It's overwhelming and I don't want to make anyone feel bad, but it makes me so uncomfortable. Louise was sup-posed to be here to help manage this . . . You have to help me. You owe me."

"Pardon?" she asked, completely shocked. "I don't owe you diddly-squat. You made my life miserable so if anyone owes anyone anything, it's you."

"That's bullshit and you know it. Come on, help me out."

"Yeah . . . no. Good luck. I'm going to go. Actually, no." She sat back down, made herself comfortable. She had no-where to go, after all. "I think I'm going to watch." She'd never seen this man so flustered. He was the coolest guy in high school, in a quiet mysterious sort of way. Nothing ever phased Brian Anderson, the emo rebel who all the girls wanted. All the girls but her.

He spoke quickly. "You don't understand. I'm not a peo-ple person. I appreciate how much they like my novels, but I can be awkward in the best of circumstances and—"

She snorted out a laugh. "Understatement of the year."

"Just do me this one small favor, please."

"Why in God's name should I help you? Just because we know each other from a long, long, loooong time ago doesn't mean we're friends. Hell, we weren't even friends back then. I kinda despise you."

"I know and I can't stand you either, but inside that evil exterior of yours there is a heart."

"For someone who writes for a living, your words are not helping you make your case, at all." She crossed her arms and watched the crowd get closer and her smile widened. "This is going to be so much fun."

"Come on, they're getting closer. Please, Lisette. Please. Your mom was the kindest women I've ever met, there has to be a shred of that kindness in you. Please."

One act of kindness . . . Those were her mother's words.

No one ever called Lizzie by her true name and hearing it from his mouth made her feel uncomfortable. It cemented the fact that there was history there; bad or good, there was something there. Her mother loved the Andersons and she always tried to see the good in little bratty Brian, as Lizzie used to call him at home. "Using my mom . . . That's a low blow, Anderson. Even for you."

"I'm desperate, Alonso," he deadpanned. "Oh . . . I know! I have a room!" he said quickly. "A huge room. It has two bedrooms. You can have one."

"What?"

"You help me and you can have a room. You can even have the bigger one with the king-size bed and its own bathroom. Fuck, Lizzie. You can have both rooms and I'll sleep on the sofa. Plllea—"

"Zeth!" A group of fans came charging toward them. They ranged from teenagers to forty-somethings and they were mostly women, although there were a couple of men too. A few of them did a strange double chin tap and swipe of the forehead with their index and middle fingers. Brian repeated the action.

What the actual cult fuck was that?

Cameras were up and selfies were being taken. For a moment she felt kind of bad for him. One fan even went as far as grabbing his face and planting a kiss right on his lips. They were invading his personal space. Even from the sidelines, she could see why he'd feel overwhelmed. Brian took a step back, trying to get a word out, but was bombarded by selfie-takers.

Years later, if asked why Lizzie said what she said next, she would chalk it up to pure exhaustion. But in the next moment, when their eyes locked, she found herself mouthing the words *I get the king bed.*

His shoulders dropped and there was visible relief pouring out of him even while the melee continued.

"When's the next book coming out?"

"Will Gwinnie and Zeth ever hook up?"

"Is the next book the last book?"

"Ladies. Ladies. Please give him some room," Lizzie said, trying to shuffle her way in among the group to get to Brian. "And no kissing the author," she singsonged.

"Hey, wait your turn," someone said, shoving her aside. Lizzie had to control her urge to elbow the offender.

"Ladies, tomorrow Brian will gladly—"

"Just one more selfie!"

"At the signing on Friday," Brian suggested, with a terrified-looking smile.

"Who the hell are you? Did you fire Louise?" someone asked sharply. "Thank God, she was awful."

"Is that your muse?" someone else asked. "She looks just like Gwinnie." The woman did the chin tap, forehead thing to Lizzie. It looked like she was trying to communicate with Lizzie in an alien language.

Lizzie shrugged and ignored the woman. "Anywho . . . I'm Lisette, I'm his new assist—" Lizzie began but Brian quickly and unnecessarily loudly spit out, "Girlfriend. Lizzie is my girlfriend. Aren't you, honey?" He put his arm around her shoulder and stiltedly pulled her close to his side.

She looked up at him with eyes the size of saucers, while his were pleading with her. She threw him a mental *what the fuck* and willed him to read her mind. But he didn't budge nor remove that stupid fake smile; instead, he gave her a little squeeze.

Everyone seemed disappointed but she had no choice but to play along or reveal the truth. Unfortunately, even if Lizzie hated Brian, she couldn't do that to him.

There were some green-eyed monsters staring back at them in surprise; he was, after all, one of the most eligible bachelors, according to *People* magazine. And apparently now he was her boyfriend.

Chapter Three

Lizzie

irlfriend!" one older woman seethed.

"Y-yes," Brian said, sounding unsure, but then he took Lizzie's hand and moved it up to his lips. To her credit, he'd shocked Lizzie so much that she let him take her hand and kiss her knuckles. "Isn't that right, sweetie?"

Lizzie looked into his pleading eyes and then the other eyes around her, staring at her, wide-eyed. How'd she get herself into this mess? It was as if everyone were holding their collective breath.

"Uh . . . yessss." She pulled their joined hands into the air like a fist pump and then, realizing how silly that was, she dropped them. "We hope you all understand. I know how deeply you all love Ziff—"

"Zeth," Brian whispered.

"Zeth, but this is Brian, and Brian and I are together. Zeth, well, he's still out there searching for love."

"Aren't we all," someone yelled and the group seemed to thaw at the idea.

"Aww"s and "oooh"s followed from the crowd. "She's why Gwinnie has brown eyes and hair the color of caramel, isn't she?" a man asked.

The crowd began to toss out more questions: "Are you left-handed? Are pineapples your favorite fruit? Are you allergic to shellfish?"

Although well-intentioned, the questions were a lot. Brian squeezed her hand and tried to answer the man's question. "No. No. I mean—" he began, but his voice was gruff and his hand was getting clammy.

"Sorry, everyone, I have to take Brian from you, but you'll see him soon. I promise." Lizzie needed to help him, as per their deal, but also he looked like he was about to throw up. How could it be that this big strong man who she remembered as being super popular in school was afraid of crowds? Yes, he was always a bit on the outside of things, more reserved than the others, but he also always went to the cool-kids parties and had the prettiest girlfriends. She'd always thought of him as confident, even if he wasn't the loudest, most outspoken person. Perhaps her perception of him had been wrong.

She had a shit-ton of questions and not to mention—

girlfriend? Why would he spit that out? She needed to kick his ass for that.

There were more "aww"s and "ooh"s as the group began to disperse.

"You wrote a character based on me?"

"Absolutely not. Brown hair and brown eyes are pretty common traits."

"Sure," she said playfully.

He shrugged and she realized they were still holding hands. She looked back and the group was still staring.

"And why would you say I'm your girlfriend? That was stupid. I was going to say assistant but you went and made this big ol' mess and— Holy shit, Anderson!" Lizzie let go of his hand when they reached the villa. "This is ginormous. How famous are you, exactly?" Lizzie said, peeking around every corner. Maybe she could pretend to hold hands a few times with him, after all.

"I know. It's ridiculous. I didn't ask for it," he replied. "A regular room would have sufficed. Let me just grab my stuff out of the master and then it's all yours."

"It's fine, I'll take the other room. It has a better view, anyway," she said. "As I was saying before your room interrupted my train of thought: 'girlfriend' was overkill and definitely outside my acting abilities. What are you going to do after the signing? What if people see us around the resort not together? And what is with the weird chin-tapping thing?"

He dropped down on the sofa and put his feet on the table. "In the books, that's how people greet each other." He did the sign, which she mimicked. "As far as why we're not always together, you're relaxing by the pool or you have a headache. Couples don't have to be together twenty-four seven. As far as after the signing, we decided we moved too quickly in the relationship and it was a mistake. And then I'll never agree to another one of these events ever again, and everything will be just fine."

"Seems like it's the opposite of fine, but not my business. So long as you don't fall in love with me."

She plopped down on the seat across from him.

"I think I can contain myself," Brian said.

"So you're B. Anderson. I've seen your books and name everywhere but it never occurred to me it was you. In fact, I thought it was a woman author. Why the anonymity?"

"I . . . it . . . " He didn't look comfortable with what he was about to say and Lizzie, who felt a constant need to control things, almost put him out of his misery by changing the subject, but then Brian let out a puff of air and said, "Grandma and Grandpa helped finance college and they were so proud of my degree in biochemistry. Med school was next. But my story ideas were taking off online. An editor approached me and I sold the rights. I didn't think it would be this big monster it turned out to be, but nevertheless, I decided on a pen name. It took me out of the spotlight as much as possible, not that I thought I'd need that when I signed the book deal."

"Knowing Mr. and Mrs. Anderson, they would've been proud."

"Deciding not to go to medical school to focus on writing would have killed them."

"I doubt that. You hung the moon in their eyes."

"Actually, you hung the moon in their eyes. 'Lizzie is so smart. Lizzie is so popular. Lizzie. Lizzie. Lizzie.'"

"Well, they were smart people. I always did like them." He shook his head, stifling a smile. "I was very sorry to hear of their passing." She'd been away at college and had heard from Marianna's mom. "I sent flowers. I know flowers don't help but I wasn't sure how to reach you and give you my proper condolences. I didn't even know if you wanted them."

"I got the flowers," he said. "I'm sure you could've reached me if you really wanted to." He said it in a mocking tone, knowing she hadn't really wanted to talk to him just like he hadn't wanted to talk to her. They weren't friends. But the passing of his grandparents had meant something to her, regardless of their relationship with each other.

"And what happened with medical school?"

"They died a few months before I was supposed to start. First Grandpa and a month later Grandma. I wasn't in the headspace for school, even if I had wanted to go. So, I wrote more. I dove into writing and pumped out book two, seven months ahead of schedule. I never went back to school and I never changed my pen name."

"Damn. Well, I know they would have been proud."

He shrugged.

"They were the best. I always did wonder how you were

related to them," she said, trying to make him smile. She didn't like the change in his voice when he spoke about them.

He grabbed a decorative pillow and tossed it at her, but she ducked before it could hit her. They both chuckled but the air had changed.

"I haven't sat down to read a book in ages. They're romance, right? I didn't take you for a romantic." *I mean, you did ruin all my Valentine's Days growing up.*

"No. Not intentionally. I've actually been told I'm the antithesis of romantic on more than one occasion."

"Maybe you are in your personal life, but seems like you write love stories, according to the interwebs."

"I don't. My books are set thousands of years in the future and seven generations after an asteroid hit Earth. In the first books, I alluded to Gwinnie and Zeth having a crush on each other and that set my readers into a frenzy. In book two, the flirtation grows but it's just a secondary plot point. The book's about the survival of a group of teenagers in the dystopian universe I created but the fans were rabid about the love story, so I've made that a bigger plotline with every book, while still sticking to the premise. Some days it seems that's all some readers want to know. 'Will Gwinnie and Zeth hook up?'"

"We live in weird times. People want a happy ending."

"Not everyone gets a happy ending in life."

"But your books are not real life. They're an escape," she said. "And after nine books, you still haven't given the fans the love story they crave."

"No. There's flirtation. I don't want this to become a love story. Once they finally get together, there won't be anything left to write."

"People continue living after they fall in love."

"But do they keep living happily? You go about your mundane life. The passion and the desire fizzle out and you're left with DVR movies and arguments over what to order for dinner."

"Super specific."

He shrugged. It seemed to her that little Brian Anderson was still the same broody kid she'd known all those years ago. One that hated love. He was a man trying to ruin love stories, just like he loved to ruin Valentine's Day.

"Well, I don't care what you do in your books, you better not try and ruin my weekend."

"Why would I do that?"

"Hellooo! Have you seen a calendar? It's February and if there's one thing I know about you it's that you will do anything to ruin my Valentine's Day. Except this time it isn't my Valentine's Day, you'd be ruining Mari's wedding."

"We're not ten years old, I wouldn't do anything to ruin your friend's wedding, just like I didn't do anything to purposely ruin your Valentine's Days."

"Yeah . . . whatever." She stood up after her eyes teared from yawning. "This day has lasted seven hundred hours and I need to sleep. I'm on London time. I can't go into past traumas at the moment. We can tackle those tomorrow."

He chuckled. "Have a good night."

She yawned again. "You too."

TWO GREEN ALIENS running toward each other in a barren wasteland. They hug fiercely as if it's been years since they'd seen each other. Their lips meet and what's supposed to be a soft reunion turns into a lashing of tongues and groping, his webbed fingers are gripping the latex of her top in a frenzy to remove it and . . .

Lizzie shot up to a sitting a position. *What the fuck? Where am I?* Kicking off the comforter with one foot, she looked around the big hotel room.

Cancún. Brian. Wedding. Jet lag.

She plopped back down on the bed and reached around for her phone and squinted into the screen.

4:42 A.M. *Shit.*

It was going to be a long day because after the weirdly erotic dream she just had, she would not be able to go back to sleep now.

LIZZIE SAT IN the lobby coffee shop, nursing her second café con leche of the morning. Everywhere she turned there were posters for the Invaders series. The resort was packed.

She lifted her café to her lips and for the first time noticed the paper cup wasn't marked with the hotel logo. It was an ad for the Invader series by B. Anderson, "soon to be a major motion picture." She rolled her eyes. Brian was everywhere.

In frustration, she stood, tossed the empty cup into the wastebasket, and decided that she would change into her swimsuit and lie out by the pool until she heard from Mari, who was supposed to arrive later today. Anything to get away from Brian's face, the eyes of which seemed to be following her everywhere she went.

"Lisette? Mija, is that you?"

She turned to see an older couple, the woman in aqua-colored linen capris and matching top and the man in a white guayabera with khaki linen pants. She recognized them immediately. They were Mari's parents.

The women pulled down her glasses. "Mira, Ramon, it's Lisette."

"Maria, Ramon! How are you?" Lizzie asked, walking toward them for a hug. It had been years since she'd seen them in person. They were family. Maria FaceTimed her weekly and worried about her in London "sola" without "familia or a novio" to care for her.

"You look so good," Maria said to Lizzie.

"Me? Look at you! You two look just like the day I met you."

"Ha!" Ramon said. "You're a sweet girl, Lisette."

"Oh, mija, we've missed you," Maria said, bringing Lizzie back into a tight hug.

"I've missed you too," Lizzie said, a lump getting stuck in the back of her throat. Maria reminded Lizzie so much of her mother, who she thought of every single day. Lorena and Maria had been close and after Lorena died, Maria had taken her role of surrogate mama very seriously. She called, FaceTimed, sent care packages from Miami as if London were a foreign land without grocery stores. "They have tea and we're café cubano people," Maria would often say when a box of Café Bustelo would show up on her doorstep.

"Did you get a room? They told us that some guests have to go to a different hotel," Maria asked.

Why hadn't she thought about this? How would she respond? "Uh, yeah, wasn't affected by the flooding. You?" She felt terrible lying, although it wasn't so much a lie as an omission, right?

"No, but they did move Gus's parents and sister. If we stay and they have to go it's going to create so much drama for Mari, so we had our room transferred to Demi, Gus's sister. We old folks can go to the other resort."

"Took one for the team."

"Yep. How inconvenient. We are waiting on the shuttle to take us. Tía Lily is going to have a field day. She is always looking for ways to criticize and the fact that half the resort is flooded is going to give her much to talk about with her bingo friends next week."

"I told you not to invite her," Ramon argued.

"She is my sister. How am I not going to invite her?" They began to bicker and Lizzie quickly changed the subject.

"I asked the front desk about Mari's room and the venue and it's all fine," she said with a smile.

"Gracias a Dios," Maria said, and made the sign of the cross. "They should arrive at noon after a long flight; the last thing I want is for her to stress over this flooding disaster."

"Maria, the shuttle. If we miss it we'll have to wait over an hour for the next one," Ramon said, pointing to the main lobby doors. "Apúrate, mujer."

"Don't rush me, Ramon. I'm going as fast as I can." She hugged Lizzie. "See you soon. If you see Mari tell her to call me. Her phone is going straight to voicemail, she must be about to board her flight."

"Will do." Lizzie and Maria gave each other a quick kiss and then the couple walked away. They felt like home to her. Since her mother died they were the biggest reminders of home and Cuba, not that she'd ever been back to Cuba or even remembered anything about the island.

Lizzie had been born in Cuba and almost immediately her parents had fled the country with her maternal grandmother, hoping to give Lizzie a better life in America. As was too often the case, shortly after arriving, her father left them.

The stress of moving to a new country and being penniless with a newborn was too much for him to bear. According to Abuela, all he and Lorena did for six months was argue about money and work. He regretted leaving Cuba but her mother never did; she knew if they worked hard enough it would eventually pay off, or at the least, America couldn't be worse than the poverty-ridden island.

Unfortunately, one day Lizzie's father just packed his

bags and left. He could have walked out on her mother and still kept in touch with his daughter, but he left them both. She wouldn't even be able to pick him out of a lineup. But her mother worked hard, always with two or even three jobs, and made it work. In fact, Lizzie only realized they were poor when other kids pointed it out in later years. And seeing Maria and Ramon reminded her of those simpler times in Miami, when they'd have sleepovers and barbecues and big Noche Buena parties together on Christmas Eve.

And now Mari was getting married, Lizzie knew that things would change. It was inevitable. It was part of life. The little she got to see her best friend now would be less once Mari had a husband and eventually kids. And if Lizzie stayed overseas, eventually they would drift apart completely, which was one of her greatest fears.

The wedding had brought them closer in the last month. Mari would call her to vent and Lizzie would console her. According to Mari, it was supposed to be a small wedding. The parents and siblings only. Unfortunately, Mari's mother wouldn't have it and insisted on the cousins and aunts and uncles. They reached a compromise and Tía Lily was included. Tía Lily was awesome and she was Mari's favorite relative (and Lizzie's too). The woman was in her eighties. Always had red lipstick that somehow ended up streaked across her teeth. She had short coiffed white hair cemented in place by large doses of Aqua Net. She always dressed as if she were going to meet someone very important, always had on her best pearls and broach. And most amusingly, she criticized everything. *Everything.* She was a nondiscriminatory criticizer. But for some reason, you never felt insulted by Tía Lily. Mostly she was a straight shooter and adored everyone, even if she said cringeworthy things to anyone she came across. Lizzie hadn't seen Tía Lily in years and she was looking forward to the train wreck she'd surely leave in her wake.

Lizzie went to the pool area, which was surprisingly empty, considering how many people were in the resort. She picked a lounge chair by the bar and dug into her bag for sunblock. After applying a thick coat, she laid down and started scrolling through her emails from her phone. William's face popped on her screen and excitedly, she smiled and swiped the FaceTime icon.

"Why are you working?" he said breathlessly. He was in the office by the looks of it and was walking toward Lizzie's office.

"I needed to reply to the emails from St. James."

"I'd already done that," he said.

"But I needed to add a few details."

"No, you didn't. My response was perfection."

She stuck out her tongue at him. It actually was perfect.

"You're the only person I know who gets bored on vacation," he said.

"I'm not bored, and I'm not on vacation. I'm waiting for Mari and I had my phone and—"

"I don't want to talk about work. I'm here . . . working. Let me live vicariously through you. Tell me about Mexico

and about that god-awful hat. Most people take glamorous floppy hats by the pool and you chose that eyesore. I
don't remember helping you pack that."

She flipped onto her stomach and rested the phone on
the lounge chair using her case. "Shut it," she said with a
smile. "So, funny story . . . you know those Invader books?"

"Duh!" he said. "Gwinnie and Zeth 4-eva!"

She shook her head and chuckled. "Well, long story
short, the author is a childhood—" She wasn't sure what
word to use. He wasn't a childhood friend. "Someone I
used to know."

"Okay," he said, uncertain.

"There was an issue with my room, well, the hotel got
flooded, and I was going to be moved to another hotel and
anyway, Brian is here for a press thing for the movie coming out in a few months but he doesn't feel comfortable in
front of large groups of people and—"

"Honey, if this is the short version—"

"The point is, he was given this humongous villa and
in exchange for my help, he let me stay there. It's ah-mah-
zing, Will. The beach is right there and the kitchen is fully
stocked. I have a four-poster bed with mosquito netting, not
that there is a single mosquito in there, but it's gorgeous."

"I feel like there's a huge plot hole in your short but
long-ass story. How are you helping him? Are you sleeping with him? How did I not know you were friends with
B. fucking Anderson! OMG . . . is this a Cancún fling!"
His voice became three octaves higher. "What happens in

Cancún hopefully continues in London! Is Brad Kilpatrick there? Violet Gram? I'm quitting and taking a flight—"

She laughed. "You're not quitting, so you can stop talking crazy."

"I need more info than that."

"We are not sleeping together. It's a two-bedroom villa. We have separate rooms. It's just pretend. I didn't know he was B. Anderson. Anderson is a common name."

"What is the exact nature of the pretend?"

Lizzie covered her eyes with the palms of her hands, dreading the words she was about to say. "I'm sorta pretending he's my boyfriend. He just needed to get some overzealous fans off his back and," she lowered her voice even further, "I don't know about Brad but Violet is supposed to be coming and she's been trying to seduce him and he's too nice to stop it."

"A real sacrifice on his part." Will snickered.

"I said the same thing. But if he has a pretend girlfriend, maybe she'll get the hint."

"Uh . . . super weird."

"It's not sounding as benign as it really is," she said.

"Lizzie!" A yelp from the other side of the pool startled her.

"Oh my God, it's Mari. She's early. Call you later. Love you," she said to William, as she awkwardly stood from the lounge chair. "Mari! You're here. You're early!"

The two women ran around the pool with open arms. It had been too long since they'd seen each other in person. "You look so good!" Lizzie said to Mari while hugging her.

"You too! I hate that I haven't seen your face in so long," Mari said.

"I know," Lizzie agreed, locking her friend in another embrace. There was a cough from behind Mari; without even having to look, Lizzie knew it was Gus, Mari's fiancé. "You get to have her every day, it's my turn. Go away," Lizzie said, playfully before letting her friend go.

"It's great to see you again, Lizzie," Gus said and took Lizzie into a warm embrace. She'd only met him face-to-face once, even though they'd seen each other on FaceTime and Skype on a number of occasions, but it wasn't the same as in person. He was a great guy and treated Mari like she was a princess. If she had to lose her best friend, she was delighted it was to Gus.

"I am so happy for you both," Lizzie said and felt the back of her throat close up. Mari was the closest thing she had to a sister and seeing her best friend so happy made her happy.

"I hope you weren't affected by the flooding. Some guests were moved to another hotel," Gus said.

"I was but . . . well, it's a story for another time. I'm staying here too. Maybe once you settle in we can meet for drinks, catch up and I'll fill you in."

"Sounds like a plan," Mari said and then hesitantly added, "I have something to tell you too." She looked around as if making sure no one was listening.

"Honey, did you check if Demi is here or in the other hotel? You know that she's dying to freshen up and, well, you know how she is," Gus said with dry sarcasm, air-quoting "dying." "Where is she anyway?"

"Probably contouring," Mari said under her breath, then smiled at her fiancé. "I checked and she's here in this hotel. Maria and Ramon gave them their room, which was a suite that was unaffected by the damage."

"Great," Gus said.

Mari didn't love Gus's sister; Demi was an influencer and was always on TikTok doing makeup tutorials and, of course, critiquing Mari's makeup. This was part of the vent sessions they'd recently had over FaceTime and cocktails. "Anyway, listen." Mari leaned closer to tell Lizzie something but it was apparently too late. "Shit, I apologize in advance," she said.

"Jason?" Lizzie said, as her ex-boyfriend walked closer to the group. "What are you doing here?"

"That's what I was going to tell you," Mari whispered. "That's Demi's wedding date."

Lizzie's eyes opened wide and Mari added, "I didn't know. She had a plus-one and had just broken up with some douche and I thought she'd be coming alone, or at least that was everyone's wish, but instead—Jason. I don't even know how they met. I'm so sorry, Lizzie. If I would have known . . ."

"Don't worry. It's fine. So fine," Lizzie lied but it was supposed to be Mari's weekend and she wasn't going to show her best friend how affected she was at seeing her ex. Her ex, with another woman. In Mexico, looking really good in beige linen pants and a white button shirt, the top buttons unbuttoned, his blond hair tied up messily on his head and a five o'clock shadow that was at around eight o'clock now.

"Hey, Iz. What are the odds, right?" Jason said when he reached her. "When we boarded the plane and I saw Mari, I was surprised." The familiar zing tore through her when he pulled her by the waist toward him and gave her a kiss on the cheek. He was a touchy sort and shit . . . she missed being touched.

She probably would have zinged at anyone, she thought.

"Jason, it's nice seeing you," she replied cordially, taking a step back and then turning to the beautiful woman by his side. "And you must be Demi, I've heard a lot about you," she said.

"Iz, wow, it's so wonderful to finally meet you! Mari speaks about you all the time."

Fuck, the woman was sweet and cute and just . . . ugh.

"It's Lisette or Lizzie, actually," Mari corrected her almost-sister-in-law. "She hates 'Iz.'"

God, Lizzie loved her best friend.

"Is it weird that Jason's here?" Demi asked, wrapping her arm around Jason's waist. "I'd hate to see my ex-bf with someone else."

"No," Lizzie said quickly, waving her hand around. "No," she repeated, her voice higher pitched than normal. "Not at all. It's been like ten years since we broke up. All water under the bridge."

"But you're here alone and Jason is here with me," Demi whispered and made a cringe-like face. It felt snarky and mean-girly, and Lizzie didn't appreciate it at all. "I would die," Demi added.

"I'm not going to die," she said, as overly dramatic as Demi. "Besides, I'm not alone." Maybe Mari was right about Demi. She wasn't all that sweet or authentic. It was all for the Gram.

"You're not?" Mari said, surprised.

"Uh . . . nope. That's what I was going to talk to you about."

"You brought a date?" Mari asked again. Lizzie widened her eyes, trying to will her best friend to stop acting surprised and definitely stop asking questions. When had they stopped reading each other's minds?

Jason had been the only man she'd ever said "I love you" to. It was in her mid-twenties and they'd dated for nearly two years before she found him in bed with another woman. She had been heartbroken and ended things as she always did—in drastic and finite form. She moved out, changed numbers, blocked his emails, packed his shit and dropped it off at his mother's house, and never ever saw or spoke to him again. She was a cut-and-dried kind of person. If it quacked like a duck . . . the man would always be a duck and she wasn't going to waste one more day on him or whatever excuse he had for cheating on her. That's not to say she hadn't been shattered. The depression was long and painful but she'd survived. Or so she thought. Maybe she'd merely pushed the pain back into a little crevice because seeing Jason again made her heart crack open.

She was saved, partly, when an overzealous photographer yelled, "Group photos!"

"That's Domingo, he's going to be taking photos," Mari said to the group.

"Ladies, make sure you glam every time you leave the room. These photos are forever. I can give you some pointers anytime," Demi said to the "ladies," who were only Lizzie and Mari. Mari literally bit her bottom lip and Lizzie pinched the base of her nose.

"You look great, Iz. So great. Maybe we can catch up later?" Jason asked, catching her off guard. "Sorry, I meant Lizzie. Since when have you not liked 'Iz'?"

"Since never. I never liked it. I used to tell you all the time." She hated when people called her Iz. She couldn't recall if it was because he always used to call her that or if it was something pre-Jason.

"Seriously?" He had a surfer-dude twang when he spoke. "Don't remember that. Anyway, about that drink?"

"Nah, I'm good, thanks," Lizzie said, sidestepping Jason and walking toward the photographer, who was trying to get the small group in perfect-picture form.

"Since you're the only one alone, why don't you sit?" Domingo said. Gus's best friend/best man hadn't arrived yet, so she was, in fact, the odd one. It felt humiliating, especially since the other couples were in beautiful linen clothes, a little wrinkled from the flight, but still perfectly put together, while Lizzie had on a muumuu-looking cover-up and her hair was in an old bucket hat. She hadn't expected to see anyone yet.

"I think I'll stay out of these photos," she said, moving away, but Mari grabbed her and pulled her in.

"No, please stay. Please."

"No, no. These photos are forever, Mari," Lizzie said, echoing Demi's words, and Mari laughed and shook her head dismissively. "I can't be immortalized looking like this." Lizzie must've looked as bad as she knew she looked because Mari agreed to let her sit out of the photos.

The next thirty minutes or so were mostly Demi and Mari talking over each other as the photographer tried to get some "candid" shots. "You okay?" Mari asked at some point while the guys were in a group shot.

"Just surprised and still jet-lagged," Lizzie said.

"I'm so sorry. I can talk with Gus so he can talk to Demi if you want and—"

"No. It's fine. I'm fine. Don't even think about it anymore. We're adults."

A young girl, maybe ten, walked by at that very moment. She looked slightly familiar but Lizzie couldn't figure out why. "Hi!"

"Hi," Lizzie said, looking confusedly at Mari.

"Can I have your autograph?" The little girl did the chin-tap-greeting thing. She had a thick accent but Lizzie didn't revert to Spanish since the girl was clearly trying her hardest to talk to Lizzie in English.

"Mi amor, leave the poor lady alone. I'm sorry. My daughter's just such a huge fan of Gwinnie." The mom said this in Spanish.

Lizzie understood that the little girl must've been in yesterday's group of fans. "That's the thing I have to tell you," Lizzie said to Mari from the corner of her mouth but then turned to the girl. "I am flattered but I'm not . . . that's not me. I'd feel uncomfortable with the autograph." The girl frowned and Lizzie quickly added, "But I'm sure Brian can give you an autograph or photo or whatever. What's your name?"

"I'm Rocio Juarez."

"Nice to meet you, Rocio. I'm Lizzie. What room are you in and I'll make sure to have some things sent to you."

"Oh . . . uh . . . we're actually staying with family but we'll be at the signing Friday night."

"Then I'll see you on Friday, Rocio. I'll make sure Brian knows to expect his most special fan to be there."

"Yeah?" She was dressed in all purple and had whiskers and a unicorn horn, likely imitating a character from the book series. Something made at home, by the looks of the threadbare pants.

"Yes, sure."

"That would be totally awesome!" the girl said.

"Gracias," the mom said sweetly. "Come on, mi amor. We'll see her and Mr. Anderson around soon." The mom pulled the girl away. Lizzie's heart bottomed out as the look of confusion spread on Mariana's face.

Mariana entwined her arm around Lizzie's and led her away from the group. "Later is now. Explain."

"Remember Brian Anderson?"

"Asshole Anderson? Neighbor from hell Anderson? Ruined your formative years and stood you up at prom Anderson?"

"Yes, yes, yes, and yes," she said. "He sat next to me on the plane. Turns out he's B. Anderson, the author."

"Shut. The. Fuck. Up," Mari said, open-mouthed. "He's the author of the Invaders series?"

"Yep."

"She thinks you're Gwinnie, as in Gwenatha X27?"

Lizzie shrugged. "I, uh . . . I guess. I didn't know that was her full name, actually."

Mari's mouth was still hanging open. She'd forgotten how big of a reader Mari was. "Are the books really that good?"

"Girl . . . Yes! The author is an enigma. Never does interviews."

"Well, it's Brian, if you can believe it. And somehow his fans seem to think I look like that character. They think I'm his muse."

"Pft. He hates you," Mari said.

"I know!" she retorted.

"But now that you say it, the character does look like you."

"Because she has brown hair and brown eyes? Those are common traits," Lizzie said, repeating Brian's words.

"But also the character's spunk. Her dimples. Yep, there's definitely something reminiscent of you. I'd have to read it again with you in mind though."

"Please don't. Anyway, there's a book thing happening at the resort this weekend and he has a signing but has major issues with crowds and one thing led to another and I'm his pretend girlfriend."

"What?"

"I needed a room. It was late. I was tired. The ride to the other hotel takes forever and they gave him a villa with two bedrooms and in exchange for the pretending, he let me stay in his room. And Mari . . . it's awesome. It has private access to the beach!"

"Super weird."

"The beach access?"

"No! Everything else. You should say yes and then stand his ass up, like he did to you!"

"You're a devious woman, Mariana." They both laughed and for a brief moment Lizzie thought of the fun it would be to get Brian back after all these years. It would be the ultimate payback. She'd never actually do something like that, but it was exciting to imagine. "I know it's all super weird. It just sort of happened but to be honest, now that Jason's here, it may work to my advantage. I don't want him to think I'm some sort of sad single woman."

Mariana was never without words, but she seemed speechless.

"Say something."

"I mean, you and Brian dating wouldn't have been far-fetched twenty years ago, but now, in a farce, it's . . . yeah . . . still no words."

"Those actually are words. What do you mean it wouldn't have been far-fetched? We hated each other. Despised. He ruined everything when we were growing up."

"You know the boy pulls the girl's hair in the playground because he has a crush on her, right?"

"When you're like five. We fought all the time. Even at eighteen years old."

"Boys mature slower."

"Mariana! There is no way that Brian Anderson had a crush on me. Impossible."

"Not only is it not impossible, but you did too."

"I did too, what?"

"Have a crush. Girl, keep up. You two had ten years of foreplay, fifteen years of seeing what's out there, and this is the reunion part."

"Oh my God. You're clearly in wedding and romance mode and aren't thinking clearly."

"So how does he look?"

Lizzie's cheeks flamed a bit.

"You're blushing. I don't think I've ever seen you blush."

Lizzie locked her arm around Mari's elbow and moved her farther from the group while looking around to make sure they were alone. "I didn't have a crush on him. I still don't." But then in a whisper she added, "But he's so fuckin' hot now, Mari. He's tall and has muscles. He wears these black-rimmed glasses that make him look sexy with a side of nerd. I think I saw a tattoo on his neck but I'm not sure."

"He wasn't ugly back then. He was just . . . Brian. The asshole."

"He's probably still just Brian the asshole but he's also Brian the brawny sexy author guy."

"You know . . . what happens in Cancún stays in Cancún."

"That's not a thing."

"Sure it is. Let's make it a thing. You're sharing a room and you're pretending to date. You could have a fling. Is he married? Dating?"

"I don't think so. Violet Gram is into him too, by the way. I can't compete with that, not that I'd want to . . . Oh my God, why am I even entertaining this suggestion?"

"Because you like him. And Violet Gram has a thing with all her costars. Don't you pay attention to TMZ? Is he into her?"

"He says he's not but shit . . . she's gorgeous and rich and she's Violet Gram!"

A loud laugh from across the pool caused both women to turn. Jason was whispering something to Demi that caused her to laugh. He tucked a piece of hair behind her ear and then kissed her. Ugh. That was his signature move. Hair tuck and kiss.

There was a time Lizzie would become weak in the knees every time he looked at her and did it. "Shit, Lizzie. I'm sorry. That has to sting."

It did. A lot, in fact. "Nah, I'm over that," she croaked, but Mariana knew her enough to know that she was full of shit. It was going to be a super-long weekend if she was going to have to witness Jason and Demi the entire time.

But wasn't that just par for the course for a Valentine's Day weekend?

Chapter Four

Lizzie

It was midday when Lizzie walked back into the villa. Goose bumps erupted on her body with the shift from the outside heat to the air-conditioned interior.

"You're up," Brian said from the kitchen.

"Been up since four in the morning," she said, dropping her beach bag and annoyance at seeing Jason by the door.

"Jet lag sucks," he said as she rounded the hall and watched him pour water into a glass.

"Indeed," she said as she took him in. Holy crap. She tried to avoid looking at him but it was nearly impossible. He wore loose checkered pajama pants and no shirt. She almost crashed into the counter at the sight. He did, in fact, have a tattoo. It was on his collarbone and crept up to his neck an inch. A symbol she didn't recognize. He was tan and there were, in fact, muscles, as she'd suspected. Not, however, the kind of muscles you got from lifting weights, but the kind of muscles you got from physical work.

"You're staring," he said cockily.

She cleared her throat and prayed she wasn't turning red at being caught ogling. "Oh, please. You wish." It didn't have the intended umph. "What's that?"

He rubbed his palm around the area of his tattoo, where her eyes were staring. "It's the sign for Earth in my books," he said before padding to his room to put on a T-shirt.

"By the way, there was a little girl who wanted my autograph. It was weird."

"Isn't it?" He returned, gulping down the glass of water in one sip and then swiping his lips with the back of his hand.

"It isn't weird for you to do it. You wrote the book! It's weird for me, since I didn't. The mom called me Gwinnie. I promised her you'd autograph her book but you should also do something special for her. She was so smitten. It was very sweet. Her name's Rocio."

"Cool. I'll set something up for her on Friday." He put down his glass and went to the table, where she noticed some boxes.

"What's all this?" she asked, watching him open a huge box with a knife.

"Just got a shipment of books and I need to sign them. It's for some auction thing they're doing on Sunday morning."

"There must be a hundred books."

"Two hundred and fifty and there's two more boxes in the other room."

"Whoa. Well, have fun with that, I'm going to shower."

Brian

Brian let out a breath when she left the room. It was difficult to keep up the pretense of hating her when her nipples were puckering through the gauzy material of whatever the hell it was that she wore. He really liked that she had short hair now because she had a long elegant neck that he wanted to nuzzle. He didn't know when his feelings had gone from disdain to neck nuzzling, but here he was, thinking with his dick.

Her gorgeous face had never been classically beautiful, yet her features together made her look a little like a pretty porcelain doll.

The fucked-up part of it all was that the snarkier she got, the harder he got. Verbally sparring with Lizzie turned him on. Maybe he needed therapy because that was all kinds of crazy. He didn't do love. People he loved tended to leave him. His parents, his grandparents, and his ex-wife. Loving was too painful.

When he was younger and people realized he lived with his grandparents because his parents had died, they treated him with kid gloves. Everyone felt sorry for him and would look at him with pity. Not Lizzie. Never Lizzie. Goading her was the highlight of his days, and the girl gave it right back to him, never missing a beat. It was the only time she directed her attention to him. Her face, neck, and the tips of her ears would get pink, and she would curse at him in a mix of English and Spanish, growing breathless with each word, her breasts heaving as she groaned in frustration. She had always stirred something in him. When they'd been young, he didn't quite know what that *something* was. Now, as a man who had had his fair share of relationships, he knew exactly what that *something* was. It was passion. It was lust. She was Lisette Alonso through and through—take it or leave it. She was a combative pain in the ass, but damn, she was a gorgeous pain in the ass. He blew out a breath, shook his head, and went back to signing the small mountain of books.

The sound of the television came from the other room a short time later. She must've finished in the shower and was changing channels over and over again. It was distracting as hell.

"Can you turn that down?" he hollered.

"No, actually I can't. Any lower and I won't be able to hear it. You need to concentrate to sign your name?"

"You're a real pain in the ass."

"Because I want to watch television?" she asked, irritated. If he wasn't mistaken the TV became even louder.

"You're in a beautiful resort; why don't you go to the pool or the beach or something. You can literally open the door, walk ten steps, and be in the ocean." He stood from the table, went to the fridge, and grabbed a beer for himself and then went to the living room. Lizzie sat right in the middle of the couch with her legs up on the coffee table. "Move over, will ya?"

She glared at him as if she weren't hogging the entire couch. "There's a chair right there," she said, pointing to a wooden chair.

Since she wasn't playing nice, he decided to sit right next to her, the entirety of their sides touching. She'd have no choice but to move or stay intimately close to him.

"Jerk," she said after a few moments, and scooted over.

"So beach? Pool? Anything but annoy me while I work?"

"Nah, I'm good."

Something was off. She was folding and unfolding a napkin she had in her hands, and the changing of channels was not because there was nothing to watch, it was because she wasn't even paying attention to the screen.

"You okay?" he asked, opening and closing his cramped hands. He had been signing the same thing over and over again and his fingers felt stiff. She turned off the television and tossed the remote onto the coffee table and stood.

He leaned forward, his elbows on his thighs, watching the

woman in white pajama-like pants and a spaghetti-strapped shirt pace around the room. Clearly, she was bothered about something but whatever it was, she wasn't going tell him. "You can tell me what's wrong, you know."

"Like you care," she said, continuing her pacing. He had to stifle a chuckle because apparently she still held that spark, even if she was preoccupied with something else.

"I guess I don't. Not really. But since, well, I am your boyfriend, I felt it was the right thing to say." It was more than that. He did care. He wasn't a bad guy so yeah, he cared. But they'd always played this game, this cat-and-mouse game. Sometimes she was the cat and sometimes she was the mouse.

He placed the bottom of the cold beer against his overused hand. She must've noticed because her brows furrowed. "What's up with you?" she asked, tipping her chin toward his hand.

"Like you care," he mimicked her earlier statement.

She gave him the finger, which made him chuckle, lightening the air between them because a moment later, she blew out a breath and finally sat back down.

"Jason, my ex-boyfriend, is here. He's Demi's date to the wedding."

"Demi?" he asked.

"The sister of the groom."

"Ouch," he said. "Was it a recent breakup?"

"Nope."

"Was it a long-term thing?"

"Two years. Longest relationship I've ever had."

"Two years is where I fall apart too."

"Really? Is that the longest you've been with someone?"

"Just about, yes. Married, actually," he said, sitting back and resting an ankle on his knee while still holding the cold beer on his hand.

"Oh," she replied, seemingly surprised by the news of his nuptials.

"Are you surprised that I was married or that I divorced?"

"Both, I guess. I don't know why. It's been fifteen years, nothing should surprise me, but damn, Anderson, you're full of surprises. You've been busy!"

He laughed heartily.

"What happened, if you don't mind me asking?"

"One day Sylvie just woke up and told me she wasn't in love with me anymore and she was leaving. She said she wanted more. I asked her what that meant, and said I'd try to give it to her, this elusive 'more.' She said if she had to explain it to me, it wasn't worth it. We didn't argue a lot, but I could tell she was unhappy that last year and nothing I did seemed to work. There was no real closure or explanation, she was just over the marriage," he said.

"How can someone be in love one day and just not be in love the next day? I don't understand that." She sounded upset at him and frankly, he didn't blame her because he'd asked himself that very question so many times. He had hated that he'd hurt Sylvie so deeply, but it also wouldn't have been fair to ask her to stay in a marriage that she just felt was . . . blah.

"I don't either but it happened. People grow apart. At first, I was hurt but now I think she did me a favor. It would have been worse to stay in a loveless marriage. She deserved more."

Lizzie seemed to mull that over for a while.

"And you? What happened with you and the guy? The ex who has you all in knots."

She shook her head from side to side as if she was in turmoil as to whether she should tell him. She swallowed a few times and for a moment he thought she'd get up and leave. "He cheated on me. I caught him. And I never spoke to him again. I guess he fell out of love too. You can't cheat on someone you love, right?"

"Is this the first time you've seen him since you broke up?"

"This is the first time I've even uttered a word to him since I caught him in bed. I threw his shit out, changed my number, and said yes to the job in London the next week."

"Wait, you didn't even have a big drawn-out fight?"

"No. Why would I? I knew I wouldn't ever forgive him, why fight over the inevitable?"

"Jesus, that's harsh," he said. It was the most vulnerable he'd ever seen her. She was fierce and independent and kept her emotions close to her heart. She was the kind of woman who he'd thought would chew up a man and spit him out, not vice versa. Seeing her this way wasn't something he was prepared for. He didn't like it and he didn't like that he didn't like it. "I'm sorry he hurt you." And he meant it. He would never have cheated on Sylvie. It would have been unfair for both of them to stay in a loveless marriage and cheating wasn't something he would ever have done.

"Pft." She straightened. "He didn't. I'm fine. Always am." She smiled and for the first time, maybe because he was seeing her with adult eyes, he realized how wrong he'd been about her. It was all a façade. Not that she wasn't a strong woman, but she also had feelings and hurts. She did care. She wasn't fine. For a brief moment, Brian felt something he hadn't felt before. Protectiveness? He wasn't sure what to call it but . . . he didn't like it. She must've noticed his expression and quickly revised her statement. "First love 'n shit. Anyway, just caught me off guard seeing him here, is all."

"I see," he said. He didn't actually see but he understood.

"Anyway." Again with the fake chirp. "Are you in a relationship now? Other than, you know, this one?" She chuckled at her own words.

"I'm not a real-relationship kinda person. This fake one is right up my alley."

"What does that even mean? You were married. You divorced and now at the ripe old age of thirty-three you're going to be single forever?"

"Pretty much. The occasional date, sex, and then everyone goes home. Uncomplicated." He took a sip of his beer and put it back on his knuckles. That's one of the reasons Violet was a problem. She was the definition of "complicated." His agent and publicist had cautioned him about this: "One bad word from her and you're canceled." But also, he couldn't be outright dismissive, they'd cautioned. He didn't know how to play the game they wanted him to play.

"That's fucked up, Anderson. I still believe in love. Even after men have repeatedly let me down—like my father, who left us just months after he and Mom stepped foot in the U.S., or Jason, who betrayed me—I still want those butterflies in my stomach, I want passion, I want the 'can't keep your hands off each other sex against the wall' romance."

"I'd never pin you for a romantic, Lizzie. You've surprised me in the last two days."

"Says the romance writer."

"Dystopian."

She stood and put her hand on his shoulder. "Keep saying that to yourself. Maybe you'll start believing it."

The last three books of the series had taken a serious turn to romance but whenever he had to take the leap and finally have the two heroes come together, he'd throw in a meteor shower or a plague-like virus overtaking the fauna and flora, causing imminent famine. His readers kept pushing for the climactic and long-awaited union of the two main characters but he'd cut the books short right before they ever got together. It just wasn't the time, even if he was receiving pressure from his readers, editor, and now the movie studio.

People wanted the fairy tale that Lizzie was talking about. Unfortunately, he didn't believe in fairy tales and his fingers couldn't seem to put the words together to make it so.

"Want to grab lunch?" he asked and almost as soon as it left his mouth he regretted it. They weren't in a real relationship and even if the hate had somewhat dissipated, they weren't friends either. "I'm just going to grab a burger from the bar. I can bring you something back. Or not." He tried to sound noncommittal.

"Thanks, but I think I'm going to take a nap."

"Not smart. If you're jet-lagged you should stay up until it's time for sleep, otherwise you're never going to get over it."

She yawned so deep it made him sleepy. "I know. But I can't keep my eyes open one more minute. I'll set an alarm. Just a quick nap."

"Suit yourself."

Lizzie

By the lack of light coming in through the balcony door, Lizzie knew it was nighttime when she woke up. Damn it, she was never going to get used to the time change if she continued taking long naps throughout the day. She did feel rested, though. She walked out of the room expecting to see Brian still signing books, but instead she saw the table with stacks and stacks of books and no Brian.

Barefooted, she walked to the table and grabbed one, paging through it. "Hope you get your wild card. B. Anderson." That's how they were all signed, in very neat blue ink.

She wondered what that meant.

She decided she'd keep one of the books. The author was her fake boyfriend, after all.

She set it aside and went for a glass of water. Unfortunately, after gulping down her drink, her stomach made a loud noise. She was going to have to leave the comfort of the villa and find herself something to eat.

She grabbed her phone and noticed a few missed texts from Mari asking if she wanted to join them for dinner. It was about an hour ago. Secretly, she was happy she'd missed the texts because spending the evening as the third wheel wasn't all that exciting.

> **Lizzie:** Sorry. I fell asleep and just woke up to your text. You're probably in the middle of dinner. Meet me at the lobby bar when you're done and we'll catch up.

She clicked send and then went back to her room, brushed her hair, applied a little bit of makeup, and decided to change from her lounge pants and camisole to a casual white linen dress. She slipped on some cute platform sandals and left in search of food.

The resort was buzzing. By the signs scattered through-out, there were smaller events going on, all book or movie related. She assumed some of the movie's supporting actors and maybe the director or producer were having press events.

"Excuse me, do you serve food at the bar?" she asked a bartender walking about.

"Sure do," he said, and she sighed gratefully.

"Thanks." She walked herself straight to the bar rather than one of the booths. She wanted to be invisible. Eat, catch up with Mari, and go back to bed. She would force herself to sleep by eleven in order to try and regulate her internal clock. That was the plan, at least.

"Buenas noches, señorita. El menú." The friendly bartender handed her the menu. "Algo para beber?"

"Si, gracias. Una margarita, por favor."

"Coming right up," the bilingual bartender said as he placed a basket of nachos and salsa in front of her. Before opening the menu, Lizzie began to nibble on chips. She was starving.

"Hey!"

Lizzie looked over her shoulder. It was Mari, who looked resort-wear chic in gauzy baby-blue palazzo pants and a flowy top that matched. Her inky-black hair was loose around her shoulders and she was wearing bright red lipstick and an envy-worthy straw bag.

"Hey you. Come. Sit." Lizzie pulled out the chair next to her and then signaled to the bartender to bring another margarita.

Click click click.

Lizzie looked over her shoulder to find Domingo taking photos of them. "You're off the clock, Domingo. No more photos tonight, please," Mari said. Domingo said his goodbyes and left.

"You look right at home here, Mari. Resort wear is your thing, girlfriend."

"Thanks!" she said. "You should have joined us for dinner. The food was delicious."

"I meant to take a short nap and I overslept. Where's Gus?"

"With his family." She made a disgusted face.

"Mari!" Lizzie said, shocked, and then looked around. "Lower your voice."

"Oh, please. There's a million people here, mariachis, music from the speakers. I can barely hear myself think. Plus, his sister's head is so far up her own ass, she couldn't hear me even if she was sitting right here next to us."

Lizzie snorted out a laugh. "Jesus, Mari, I always thought you loved his family."

"I do. It's mostly Demi and her contoured face and perfect hair and constant little digs. His mom's the best but when Demi's around the vibe changes. Why do you think I'm all decked out? Everything we do will be on TikTok by morning and I know the little witch is trying to catch me without makeup or with lettuce between my teeth or a booger coming outa my nose. Anyway, in small doses, it's controllable but we've been together most of the day. I needed distance."

She let out a deep breath, one that sounded as if she'd been holding it in for far too long. "Speaking of doses, we need a shot!" Mari declared and when Lizzie started to protest she added, "Please, Lizzie. I'm getting married this weekend! Don't say no."

"Okay. Okay," Lizzie said as the bartender brought over the margaritas. "And apparently, we'll also be ordering bad decisions," she added and the bartender's lips quirked up.

"Two shots of Patrón," Mari ordered and then turned her attention back to Lizzie. "Where's your boyfriend? Are you actually taking him to the wedding? Please don't kick him in the balls anywhere close to my cake."

"That was an accident," Lizzie said in defense of the sixth-grade incident that almost got her suspended. "We were playing kickball and I missed the ball."

"I think you hit the balls you intended to hit," Mari said, with a snort. "When you two are in the same room, disaster ensues."

"That was twenty years ago. We're mature adults now."

Mari's brow furrowed. "Well, I'm a mature adult now but you two are playing pretend so I'm not sure I'd make that analysis just yet."

Lizzie took a big sip of her drink, which seemed full of liquid again. Either the bartender had been refilling it when she hadn't been looking or she hadn't drunk much of it. Considering that she felt very relaxed all of a sudden, she knew she'd had at least one full drink.

"Oh, Liz, I've missed you so much," Mari said, her eyes becoming watery. Mariana was a sappy drunk and she'd likely had drinks at dinner, so she was teetering on sobs. She leaned over to hug Lizzie but her chair tilted forward, and she tumbled onto Lizzie.

"Oh shit!" Mari said and burst into a cry-laugh that also sent Lizzie over the edge into fits of uncontrollable laughter.

Maybe she should've eaten something.

"Uh oh!" a deep voice—a deep and familiar voice—said from nearby. "This looks like trouble."

Without even having to look up, she mumbled, "Anderson."

Mari stood and righted her stool, then sat back down while Lizzie wiped the laughter tears from her face.

"I guess you finally woke up," Brian said, looking exceptionally sexy in loose-fitting jeans and one of those rock band T-shirts. This one said *Journey* on it. She hated that she found him sexy. Apparently, she was into guys with glasses who wore rock-and-roll T-shirts. Who knew?

"Anderson, you were supposed to wake me up," she said over a hiccup. She covered her mouth and he chuckled. "One hour. That's all I was supposed to sleep."

"You never shared that plan with me," he said and she took a moment to think about that.

"Oh yeah. I thought it, though."

"I'll start reading your mind, no problem," he quipped.

"Ohhhhhh . . ." Mari said and Brian turned his attention to her. "This is so cute!"

"Mariana," he said in the form of a hello. "Congrats on the nuptials."

"Congrats on all the money and muscles," she said, wiggling a finger around his biceps area. This time he laughed out loud. "You are hot. You weren't wrong, girlfriend. You weren't wrong."

Brian gave Lizzie a pointed look. He adjusted his glasses and wiggled his brows. She rolled her eyes. "Whatever. I can still hate you even if you are sort of handsome."

"*Hot*. She said hot," he corrected her and she glared at him. "Did you have dinner?" he asked.

"Oh yeah! Tacos, I want tacos and more nachos. Oh, and guacamole. Let me find that bartender." She started to turn but her stool wobbled. Shit, she was getting a little sloppy. "These chairs are stupid."

"And dangerous," Mari said.

"Why don't you ladies go over there. I'll order you some food," Brian offered, pointing to a booth. With a knowing nod, the bartender took the drinks off the bar before either of them could protest. "I'll take their drinks over, man. You make sure they make it safely to the booth."

"It's like ten feet. We'll be fine," Lizzie said.

"They do kilometers here. I know this because my parents' hotel is like a zillion kilometers away and Gus said that was twenty miles. I would be lost without Gus. I don't know kilometers!" Again with the waterworks.

"Is she crying over the metric system?" Brian whispered to Lizzie.

"It's the alcohol, she's an emotional drinker."

"And you are?"

"Wouldn't you like to know?" she said with a sexy(ish) wink, because she hiccupped at the same time and he wasn't certain whether it was intended to be sexy.

Brian helped the ladies to the booth and then invited himself to the party.

"Anderson, guess what?" Lizzie said when she slid into the booth.

"What?" he asked, amused.

"I stole one of your books. Imma read it."

"They're so good! I don't like you, Brian Anderson. You were the biggest asshole growing up, but shit, those books were unputdownable." Mari struggled to say the word and it came out slow—syllable by syllable. "I had so much sex with Gus during book five and the scene where Gwinnie and Zeth are stuck in the cave for the week. Talk about sexual tension!"

"TMI," Lizzie said and Brian pinched the bridge of his nose.

"Can you tell me a secret, Brian?" Mari leaned over the table. "When. In. The. Ever-loving. Fuck. Will Gwinnie and Zeth fuck?"

Lizzie looked around and then shushed her friend, who was speaking too loudly. Brian shook his head and slid some water across the table to Mari, who waved it off, opting instead for more margarita.

"You'll have to keep reading to find out," Brian replied.

"You suck," she said with a pout.

"Do you think maybe you should have some water or food?" Brian said to both of them. "Eat nachos, Lizzie." He reached for the chips and tried to feed some to her but she pushed his hand aside.

"I can eat my own nachos, thank you very much!"

Fortunately, the chips did reach her mouth.

Unfortunately, however, she over-dipped the salsa and on the chip's way to her mouth, a glob of salsa fell off the chip and slid right into the cleavage of her dress.

Brian

Brian watched the red sauce slide down between her breasts. He suddenly had a strong desire to eat salsa.

"Uh oh," she said, looking down.

Brian unwrapped the utensils and handed her the cloth napkin. "Should I help?" he asked playfully but she yanked the napkin out of his hand.

"You wish," she said and he grumbled, "I do," under his breath.

How much had they drunk? They were completely wasted, Mari more so than Lizzie, but she was trailing close behind.

He couldn't stop staring at Lizzie as she reached into her

dress to clean up the mess. Her pin-straight hair that ended by her jawline was parted in the middle and tucked behind her ears. Her short white dress against that tan skin was driving him crazy. He was glad they were sitting in a booth and her legs were now hidden from his gawking.

"Since I'm a smart man, I know that I'm not going to convince you to call it a night or at the very least switch to water."

They both glared at him and Lizzie gave him the finger. She was fond of doing that.

"So, I will make you a deal. I will pay your tab, which is probably astronomical at this point, if you alternate water between drinks."

The women looked at each other and nodded.

"And food. Water and food," he added.

"Fine fine," Mari said.

Brian ordered drinks and a pitcher of water for the women, a beer for himself, and decided to stay and watch the shit show that was surely to happen if the two women continued in their current trajectory.

"Does Gus know you're here?" Lizzie asked Mari.

"Who cares."

"Let's talk about it," Lizzie said.

"No! Anderson, tequila," Mari ordered. "Lizzie talks too much. Tequila quiets her."

"Not a lie," Lizzie admitted.

He laughed. "Probably not a great idea," he said, but ordered it anyway.

"B." A group of women walked by the bar and took photos from their phones. He appreciated the attention but it just felt weird to have strangers photograph him without his permission. "Gwinnie!"

"That's you," he whispered.

Lizzie shot up and looked around. "Oh yeah! That's me!" She waved back. The group was standing away trying to be cordial by giving him his space, which he immensely appreciated, but it still felt intrusive.

"Anyway, back to your marital woes," Lizzie said.

"I don't have marital woes."

"Listen, you are lucky to be in love. You and Gus are perfect for each other. Don't argue over silliness. Like Elsa always says, 'Let it go!'" Lizzie singsonged the words and flung her arms out, hitting Brian right in the face. "Oh shit. I'm so so sorry."

She grabbed his face in her hands. "I've been told I gesticulate too much. Brits don't seem to appreciate a good Cuban gesticulation." Her hands were soft against his skin and she was looking into his eyes, softly, rubbing his cheek with her thumb.

"I think you gesticulate just the right amount," he said and then she let go of his face like it was a hot potato. When they both turned, Mari had her chin on her palm, elbows on the table, staring at them. Eyes, of course, full of unshed tears.

Lizzie rolled her own eyes.

"So, as I was saying, forgive him. He can't help it if his

sister is an ass— Oh Jesus, that is a huge rock!" She took Mariana's hand in hers and moved it back and forth. "It's bigger in person."

"That's what she said," Mariana retorted and the two women bowled over in cackles. "Here, try it on."

Mariana slipped her ring off her finger and then grabbed Lizzie's hand, forcefully. "Wait, I think that's bad luck. Ouch! Wait, stop. No. It's not fitting. Don't force it—ohhhhhh." The two women stared at the ring in awe. "So pretty."

"So so pretty," Mariana said. "He did good, right?"

"Of course he did, he picked you."

Then they were both crying and Brian wasn't sure what was happening.

"I'm so happy for you, Mari."

"And I'm happy for me. And I'm going to go have sex with Gus because it's not his fault that his sister is an asshole."

"Exactly," Lizzie said, taking her cloth napkin and dabbing her face.

"You're engaged!" The group of fans who had been walking by were now sitting at the booth next to them and they started snapping more photos from their phone.

"No. It's not—" Brian began but they were already taking selfies and instead of denying it both women smiled into the photos, posing and showing off the huge shiny ring on Lisette Alonso's finger.

What. The. Actual. Fuck.

"Rounds for all!" Lizzie said, and Brian was too stunned by the engagement situation to say anything. Luckily, "all" was the three of them and the four women who'd gone from sitting next to them to somehow sliding into their booth. By "somehow," he meant Lizzie had invited them over. "You're so lucky you get to go on girls' trips. I never get to see my Mariana anymore," she said to the group of women.

"Brian's a jealous guy?" one asked. "That's so Zeth."

"Noooo," she slurred. "I'm just in London and she's here and I never get to see her."

"I miss you. It's been forever, Lizzie. It feels like years!" Mari said.

"Wait? You live in London?" One of the women, whose name he'd learned was Loraine, asked Lizzie and then Brian.

"Uh . . . well, yeah and, uh . . ." Lizzie looked horrified at being caught in the lie.

Brian put an arm around her shoulder. "It's been difficult doing the long-distance thing. I try and fly over monthly. Plus, distance makes the heart grow fonder, isn't that right, sweetie?"

She looked at him and he squeezed her shoulder. "Uh, yes. Fonder 'n shit."

"I've been looking everywhere for you." It was Gus, who'd spotted them from the lobby, which was emptier now since most people had gone to bed.

"Oh, it's Gus! I was just leaving to have sex with you." Mari pulled him down by his neck and gave him a big loud kiss on the lips that was not quite appropriate in polite company.

When Gus was able to pull away from his fiancée, he looked at her carefully then at Lizzie. "You guys are blitzed."

"I've been trying to get them to stop," Brian said. "You must be Gus." He extended his hand to the man. "I'm Brian."

"Nice to meet you, man. Once these two start it's impossible to stop them. All we can do is stick around and hope they don't get into trouble."

"It's been interesting," Brian said.

"We flew out to London last New Year's, which is when I met Lizzie, and these two started drinking prosecco at one in the afternoon while catching up." He air-quoted "catching up." "We never got to midnight. They passed out by nine."

"Good times!" Brian said with a laugh.

"It actually was. Thanks for watching my girl." Then he turned to Mari. "Ready, babe?"

"Yup," she said as the other women slid out of the booth to let Mari out. Mari hugged each of them as if they were old friends and the women took their cue and called it a night, giving Brian and Lizzie hugs as well.

"I guess it's time to go." Lizzie slid out of the booth and wobbled. He swiftly grabbed her waist and steadied her. "Whoa," she said, gripping his forearms.

"Lizzie, sweetheart, I think it would be a great idea if you took off the heels," he said.

"Why?" She swayed again.

"One, it's a shorter fall, and two, I don't want you to break your ankle."

"Pfft, neither of that's gonna happen. I walk in heels through cobblestone streets. Cobblestone! Have you ever tried to walk in heels on cobblestone? It's nearly impossible but I do it every single day."

He held his hand out in surrender. "If you say so."

And the woman wasn't lying. She had a killer fucking walk. One that made his cock hard. One leg in front of the other as if the hallway through the resort were her own personal catwalk.

The problem was she was walking the wrong way.

"Mari is a crier and you're an even bigger pain in the ass," he said.

"Shut up," she said, walking with purpose, but no direction, around the resort.

Eventually he got tired of her hardheadedness and the twenty-minute drunk detour. He took her hand in his and she surprised him by accepting the gesture. He directed them to his villa and ignored the strange emotion holding hands with Lisette Alonso aroused in him.

Chapter Five

Lizzie

Lizzie's head was pounding hard. "Ugh." She groaned and stretched her arms wide, trying to release all the tension in her muscles.

"Fuck. Ow!" Brian said as her hand connected with his face. The gesture gave her a sense of déjà vu.

"Oh shit. I'm so sorry," she said and then winced as her head throbbed with the noise of her own voice. *Wait!* Had she just hit someone? She wasn't alone in bed. She sat up. "What the hell are you doing in my bed, Anderson?"

"You're in *my* bed, Alonso," he countered gruffly, throwing the covers off himself and sliding out of bed all while rubbing his jaw from the hit. She pulled the covers up to her shoulders as she watched him head to the bathroom.

What had she done?

She could feel the soft cotton of her sleep shirt and pants underneath the covers. Thank God she wasn't naked. She looked around the room and yes, this was in fact not her room. The memories of tequila and bad decisions whirled around her head.

"How'd I end up in your bed? I know we didn't do anything."

"What makes you so sure?" he asked from the other room.

"We despise each other, right?" She had lost track of what was real and what was make-believe. "It would be impossible to hook up with you. My vagina would surely reject your penis," she said, rubbing her temples. "I must've been confused by the rooms."

"No. No," he said through a mouthful of toothpaste from the bathroom. "You knew which room was mine. You chose to be here so perhaps you don't despise me as much as you think. And perhaps it's my penis who'd reject your vagina."

"I highly doubt that!" Lizzie kicked off the covers, threw her legs over the edge of the bed, and waited for the room to stop moving before standing up.

"Well then, you should know that I physically carried you to bed twice, and you kept coming back. 'I don't wanna be alone, Anderson. Pleaseeee . . . Anderson, hold me, Anderson.'" He mimicked a woman's voice. Luckily he was in the other room, otherwise she would surely die of mortification.

"I have never asked a man to hold me." It was true. She liked her space. She normally wore a sleep mask, had blackout curtains, a pillow between her legs, two under her head, and a white-noise machine. She liked comfort and quiet. She despised being held and feeling stifled and sweaty, her hair being tickled by the breath of a man by her ear. It was the worst kind of torture.

"Well, sweetheart, you did. A lot. So much so that I gave up and let you snuggle—your word not mine—into me. It was the only way I was going to be able to get any sleep and I was exhausted from having to babysit you all night."

The nerve of the man! "Shut up." She childishly covered her ears, unable to hear any more of the humiliating story, which was coming back into her memory bank one cringeworthy moment after the other. "Stop talking. Stop. Talking."

She stood and stomped out of the room. He was so rude. Assuming that it was as he said it was, there was no need to say it out loud. The humane thing would have been to ignore it and pretend it never happened. But that was the thing about Brian. He called her out on all her shit. Didn't let one thing slide. Yep, she still despised the ogre.

Brian

Brian heard her slam her room door shut and he snickered. He hadn't been lying, she had asked him to snuggle.

She had shuffled in after he'd gone to bed, looking adorable in her pajamas, a modest cotton blush-pink pant and shirt set, her hair a mess, and a big sweet pout on her lips, as she begged to be held. Literally, begged. His dick seemed to beg to do the holding but that had been figuratively and something he'd never share out loud.

It had been a helluva long time since he'd snuggled with a woman and Lisette Alonso had been the last woman he wanted to snuggle with. Or so he thought. In his experience someone normally hogged the covers, kicked or moved too much, or generally made him uncomfortable. Snuggling with Lizzie, however, and unfortunately, entailed softness and sweetness, which was difficult to reconcile since there was ordinarily nothing soft and sweet about Lizzie. Once he relented, she'd quickly moved in close, wiggling and worming into the crook of his shoulder, her front to his side, her arm over his chest. She felt . . . she felt . . . It started with a *p* and rhymed with "merfect." He wouldn't even think of that word in relation to the woman who made his childhood a living hell.

He must've just been horny and she was a woman, a beautiful woman, admittedly, who had been pressed close to his body. Any man would have reacted, it was normal. That's what he would continue to tell himself because this weird arrangement was temporary and he couldn't do anything as stupid and irresponsible as catch feelings for Lisette Alonso.

While she holed up in her room, he took the opportunity

to order breakfast and catch up on his emails. As he hung up with room service, he heard his name yelled. "Anderson! Anderson!"

His heart beat out of his chest as he ran into her room. *Had she fallen? Was she hurt?* Lizzie's head was sticking out of the bathroom door; water leaked down and pooled on the floor. The woman was clearly pissed off.

Awkwardly, she stuck her hand out the bathroom door and showed him the ring on her finger. He'd forgotten about that. "What the hell is this?"

He smirked, when his heart stopped pounding out of his chest, and he leaned casually against the wall, crossing his arms and ankles. "Oh, that. It's an engagement ring. Mariana's engagement ring."

"And it's on my finger because . . . "

"I don't know the because of it, but I know the effect of it."

"Effect?" she asked as she awkwardly tried to pull it off her finger while holding the door semi-closed.

"Well, because we're now engaged." He said it matter-of-factly and knowing it would piss her off even more that he wasn't freaking out. Well, outwardly that was true. Inwardly he was trying to figure out how the hell they were going to get out of this mess.

"What!" She yelled so abruptly the door opened fully and she came tumbling forward. He caught a glimpse of her naked body as he quickly moved forward to catch her.

"Let go of me," she said, even though she was holding

on to him while gathering her balance. She scurried back inside but this time grabbed a towel and wrapped it around her body.

"You're a fucking mess, you know that?" he said, because anger was better than lust in this situation.

She stepped out and poked his chest with her ringed finger. "Me? I was supposed to be here for my friend's wedding and somehow I end up dating you one day and engaged the next. This is on you!" Damn, his fake fiancée was hot. "Turn around," she ordered.

"Please," he said to the door of the bedroom. He too was starting to get upset. There was absolutely nothing wrong with being engaged to him; he was a successful man and women asked him out all the time.

Why was he even justifying such a stupid problem that wasn't even real?

"Please, what?" she asked breathlessly as she opened and closed drawers.

"Please, turn around, Brian," he said mockingly.

"Please, fuck yourself, Brian Anderson."

He laughed loudly.

There was a knock at the door. "Yoo-hoo. Señor Anderson, it's Pablo. May I come in? Hello?"

"Who the hell's Pablo?" she whispered.

"Yes, come in. Un momento, Pablo. I'll be right there!" Brian said loudly, then turned to Lizzie, who was now dressed. "The hotel provided me with someone to assist me."

"An assistant?"

"No rush. I'll just set up this food on the dining room table for you, señor," Pablo hollered back.

"A butler! You have a butler!" she whisper-yelled. "You think you can just waltz into my life and turn it upside down with your villas and butlers and ugh . . . whatever!" She wasn't making sense but he was now pissed off too. She had been the one who had been drunk and she had been the one who had not set the record straight about their engagement last night, and she had been the one to burrow into his bed to fucking snuggle. Further, she had been the one who'd been an asshole to him throughout their younger years, not vice versa. Why the hell was she so mad now?

"I didn't ask for this . . . ambassador, that's what they called him. It's weird. Makes me uncomfortable," he said, with fury, and then walked out of the room, slamming the door behind him. The woman really knew how to ruffle his normally calm feathers. He was pretty even-keeled; in fact, that was his ex-wife's favorite trait, Sylvie had once said. They never argued, mostly because he didn't feel a need. Nothing was that bad that he'd have to get worked up about. Even his divorce had been relatively uneventful. They'd both gone their separate ways, splitting everything evenly down the middle, like mature and rational adults.

"I told you yesterday, you better not fall in love with me, Anderson!"

"Trust me, that would never happen! I don't think I can

even get past the dislike!" he shouted through the door. Shouted! When was the last time he'd gotten this worked up?

"Good!"

A few days with Lizzie, and he wanted to pull his hair out. He didn't feel rational, he felt completely discombobulated; there was no way he'd ever catch real feelings for her.

With a deep breath, he stepped out to the dining area. "G'morning, Pablo."

"Buenos días, señor."

"You don't have to set this up. I got it." He would've eaten by the television.

"No. No. You sit and relax, señor," the man said as he placed food on the table. "Mimosa?" he asked, taking out a bottle of champagne from the bottom of the serving cart.

"No. No. I'm fine. Thanks. This seems like more food than I'd ordered."

"Sí. I added some complimentary pastries. Mi esposa, Matilda, works in the pastry kitchen and she made these especially for you. Pastelitos de coco, de guayaba, y de chocolate," he said with a big proud smile. "Also, the hotel is providing you with tickets for complimentary couple's massages for you and your lady friend," Pablo said with a wink. "How do you say? Not wife. Before wife. Oh . . . fiancée. For you and your fiancée lady."

Brian ran his palm down his face. The secret was already out. *Thank you, social media!*

"Are you okay, señor?"

"I'm fine, Pablo," he said and went to find his wallet. He took out some money and handed it to Pablo when the man finished setting things up. "Oh, and here, this is for your son," Brian said and reached for one of the signed hardcover books.

"Oh, thank you, señor. Thank you so much!" The man held the book against his chest as if it were the biggest treasure he possessed. Brian made a mental note to grab copies of the entire series and some swag and give it to Pablo before the weekend was over.

"Did your manservant leave?" Lizzie asked, padding her way to the kitchen.

"Pablo's gone, yes. He's not my manservant."

"I need butter. Did he bring butter?" she said as she rummaged through the table's contents and started to open all the little butter packets. She then scooped out the butter from each and every one of them with her finger and began to coat her ring finger with it.

"Why didn't you try with the soap in the shower?"

"I did, Sherlock," she said indignantly and pulled hard, whining in frustration. "It's not coming off! Argh."

"Let me see that." He took her hand in his. Her finger was slick with butter. He tried to pull but nothing happened.

"Ow," she said and yanked her hand away.

"That looks really stuck," he said and she glared at him as if he'd grown a second head.

"Thank you for that observation, Captain Obvious." She was nervously jumping in place as if standing on hot coals, while fanning the hand around, as if it were just going to slide off. "Oh my God! What do I do? Mari's getting married in two days and she needs this ring!"

He grabbed her hand, dragging her behind him to the sink. He poured a huge glob of dish soap on her hand and lathered it really well and then tried to pull again and nothing happened except that her finger was now red and swollen in the area right above the ring.

"Okay, new plan," he said, washing the soap off her hand. "Leave it alone for bit. Let the swelling go down and we'll try again in a few hours. If it swells further it could stop the circulation."

She was still pulling on the ring and he took her hands in his. "Stop touching it. It's making it worse. Maybe try not to have any more margaritas."

"I think getting drunk is the only way that will help the situation. It's not like we can get fake-engaged twice!"

"No, you nut. The salt and the alcohol are probably making you retain liquid. Drink a lot of water for the next few hours. I think that may help with the swelling."

"Oh, okay. Good plan. Let's go with that," she said hysterically. "I'm going to vomit now," she added.

He put his hands on her shoulders and looked at her softly. Compassionately. "It's going to be fine. We'll get this off even if we have to cut it off."

"Oh my God. I meant vomit from the hangover, not because of my anxiety over the ring."

"Oh." He misread that.

"And, Anderson, cutting off my finger is not an option!"

"I meant the ring, Lisette. Cutting off the ring!" He shook his head from side to side in frustration.

"I think my finger is worth less." She let out a defeated breath. "I need to find gloves or something. If anyone sees this, it's going to blow up."

Now it was his turn to blow out a big defeated breath. "Lizzie, babe, Pablo set this up for us. *Us.* As in me and you, my fiancée. He already knew, which means everyone already knows."

She plopped down on one of the dining room chairs. "Remind me why you didn't stop me from this engagement?"

"Can anyone stop Lisette Alonso from doing anything?"

"Point taken. Okay, it's fine. No big deal. It's only three more days, right? We can keep pretending. Boyfriend, fiancé, it's not a huge difference," she said. Parts of nonhysterical Lizzie were now coming to life. The fierce woman who made plans and was organized.

"We can tell your friends the truth if you want."

"About that," she said. Lizzie did something he hadn't seen her do since she was eighteen. Hell, he'd forgotten about this quirk of hers. It was the telltale sign that he'd gone too far or she was hiding something from someone.

She cleaned.

At first he thought she was just bringing the plate closer to her but as he observed, he saw she was making sure it was perfectly centered on the place mat. She took the napkin and began to absentmindedly wipe away crumbs. He knew she didn't even realize she was doing it. Her brain was working on something else. She moved the glass of juice an inch to the right, then back to the left half an inch.

He placed his hand gently over hers. "Tell me."

She looked up as if she'd forgotten he was there.

"Lizzie," he warned.

"I don't think we should tell anyone. I mean, Mari knows but that's all. Isn't it better if we keep up appearances at all times? Not when we're in here alone but when we walk out?" She unfolded the napkin and then put each corner together perfectly.

"Lizzie," he warned again.

"What? It's easier that way. That's like how actors do it 'n shit."

He just stared at her, waiting.

"Okay, fine. Maybe you can do me this tiny little favor."

"I'm currently in the middle of your first favor."

She put the napkin down and there went worried Lizzie and in walked annoyed Lizzie. "I'm doing you a favor, not vice versa," she said, pointing her forefinger at him.

"Says the lady who's sleeping in a villa overlooking the Gulf of Mexico, thanks to me."

"Ugh!" She rolled her eyes, pushed her chair back, and stood. "I don't want to argue—"

"Are you sure about that?"

She gave him the finger, and he chuckled.

"Remember how I told you that ex-boyfriend is here with Demi? It's messing with my head a little," she admitted, moving a crystal bowl on the kitchen counter to a different spot. "I don't want him to think I'm here alone. It's humiliating."

Wow. He hadn't seen that coming. It was the first time he'd seen her being . . . real. Normal. Someone who wasn't perfect.

"Seriously? You're Lisette Alonso, valedictorian, most popular girl in school. Hell, most popular girl everywhere. Since when do you give a shit about what other people think?"

"It's a long story. I just need to not be alone here. Please."

He shrugged. "Fine by me."

"Really? Because that means you'll have to go with me to the wedding. It's Saturday afternoon."

He thought about it and an interesting plan formulated in his head. He didn't even think on it before he blurted it out. "On two conditions," he said, and the glare was back. "First, you start coming with me to all my events and help keep me from saying anything stupid."

"Why me? I mean, I know I'm the only person here you know but what makes you think I can help?"

Was she serious? "You are the most talkative person I know and before you get all pissed off and take that as an insult, it's meant as a compliment. You walk into a room and hold court. It's amazing. You used to do that even back then. You know how to read a room and say the right thing. You're funny and smart and you aren't shy. I, on the other hand, become a stuttering awkward mess and never know what to say."

Her eyes were wide and her mouth opened and closed a few times. "That's the nicest thing you've ever said to me, Brian."

He shrugged.

"Okay. I can do that. What's the second condition?"

"You have to start being nice to me."

"What?"

"You heard me. If we have to convince half of this hotel that we're in love, I don't want to fake-smile and then fight with you every time we walk into this room. It's been fifteen years, Lizzie. We can be civil to each other."

"I can if you can."

He held out his hand and she took it. "Then it's a deal."

For some reason he had an ominous feeling that this wasn't going to end well no matter how many rules they made.

"And don't worry, I won't fall in love with you," he threw her words back at her.

Lizzie

He had left her utterly shocked with his words. He thought her smart and funny. Maybe he didn't exactly hate her as much as she thought he did. She had told him not to fall in love with her as a joke but it wasn't so funny anymore. She was accidently starting to like her nemesis.

Brian stood and walked to his bathroom and came back a few minutes later with two Advils, which he handed to her with some freshly squeezed orange juice. "Now, since you agreed you're going to start listening to me, please take these and eat something. It'll help you feel better."

"I didn't agree I'd listen to you. I just agreed I'd be nice," she said, taking the Advils and then sitting down to enjoy the big breakfast in front of her.

He walked away before she had a chance to thank him.

LIZZIE WAS SITTING on a lounge chair on the balcony reading Brian's book. She'd meant to read just a little while she nursed the hangover. Instead, she was two hours and five chapters into the story, hangover long forgotten. It was good. Like, really, really good. And he hadn't been lying: it wasn't romantic, at least not yet.

She was impressed at his world-building skills. He had meticulously created a world in the future filled with creative characters seeking survival in a barren land where survival seemed impossible. Zeth had not yet entered the story but Gwinnie had. Everyone was wrong about the description. Gwinnie was tall, almost six feet, whereas Lizzie was five-seven. Gwinnie had long light brown hair and Lizzie's was short, although when Brian had known her, Lizzie had had long hair. The only thing they had in common was their dimples and maybe the big brown round eyes. People were ludicrous in making the comparison.

Her phone buzzed and she answered when she saw it was Mari. "I. Am. Dying," she said and Lizzie chuckled into the phone.

"I was feeling terrible earlier too," Lizzie admitted. "Remind me that I'm allergic to tequila next time."

"We're supposed to meet the wedding planner in an hour and having a bikini wax while lying in a pit of red ants feels more inviting then leaving this room to talk with this uber-happy planner."

Lizzie laughed. "Come to my room instead. I want to catch up, sober."

Mari guffawed into the phone.

"So long as there's no tequila within a ten-mile radius," she said. "Oh, and before I forget, you have my ring. I can't believe I forgot to get it back from you. I haven't been that drunk since—"

"My going-away party five years ago."

"You are often involved in my bad decisions. You and tequila."

"And that's why you love us both."

"You got that right. See you in a minute," Mari said before ending the call.

Lizzie looked down at her still-swollen finger and tamped down the desire to tug on the ring again. How would she explain this to Mari or Gus? She needed the ring off her finger STAT.

A few minutes later Lizzie was sitting on her balcony with Mari nursing coffee. "Where's your fake fiancé?"

"Not sure. He left a while ago."

"And how's that going?"

"I think we're not going to continue faking it. Well, we're not going to get for-real married but we're not going to actively despise each other. He's actually not too bad."

"I won't tell him you said that," Mari said, propping her legs on the railing and looking out at the sea. "It was so long ago, anyway. You can surely forgive him."

She shrugged. "I have trust issues."

"You have 'staying in one place' issues, girlfriend," Mari said.

"What does that even mean?" Lizzie asked, taking a sip of her coffee. The ocean breeze was blowing softly around them. The day was gorgeous, blue skies and clear waters.

"It means that you run away when things get a little uncomfortable."

"That's not true. I had a job opportunity in London, I didn't run away."

"Oh, puleaze. You had job offers in Miami too. I love you anyway, but you could have stayed. You ghosted me for two months after that."

Mari started to change the subject to something wedding related, as if she'd not just dropped a verbal grenade. Lizzie hadn't meant to ghost her friend and they'd had a big fight after that. She'd just been so depressed, she hadn't wanted to talk to anyone. She'd apologized a dozen times for that.

"Uh . . . excuse me? I didn't know you felt that way."

"I didn't know you didn't know this about yourself," Mari said.

Lizzie sat back and closed her eyes and thought about what her friend was saying.

"Remember how you changed from world history to AP civics because Karen Da Silva was in world history. Or how you decided to go to FSU when you could've just stayed at UM after your grandmother passed away and then a few years later when your mother passed away . . . well, London," Mari added. "Lizzie, this is not a critique, I swear, it's just something you've always done. You make a clean cut and walk away."

Is that what her best friend thought of her? Lizzie's eyes teared up but she didn't let the tears fall.

"Oh shit!" Mari said, dropping her foot from the railing. "I broke you. I'm sorry. It's not bad. I envy you. You make decisions and stick with them while I take forever to decide on everything. That's really brave and bold, Lizzie. I just wish you weren't so far away, is all."

She hadn't been running away. All those examples were merely coincidences. She had a scholarship to FSU, that's why she'd left. Well, she'd had one to UM too. And London was a no-brainer, a great opportunity. Wasn't it?

"I didn't appreciate being cheated on by Jason or being

dumped by Rob before that, the string of shitty boyfriends, or my mom passing away."

"Having shitty boyfriends is, unfortunately, part of life. How would you know when the perfect one comes along if you don't have the shit ones as comparison?"

Lizzie tried to smile.

"I'm no psychologist but I think talking about it is the healthy thing to do. Not leaving the scene like you committed a crime."

Needing to think this through later, Lizzie changed the subject. "So tell me about you? Are you excited? Scared?"

"I'm mostly worried. Will the best man show? What if it rains? What if Gus gets cold feet? What if you decide to claw Jason's eyes out? Like I said, it's not healthy to bottle things up. I'm waiting on the other shoe to drop and the shoe being—you going crazy on Jason's face."

"If the best man doesn't show up, who cares? If it rains, we'll move it inside. And if there is one thing I know for sure, Gus will show up. He adores you. And I have great skills at suppressing my emotions. I wouldn't do anything that nuts at your wedding."

"Aw, Lizzie, I've missed you!" Mari said, leaning over to hug her. "Oh shit, my ring?" she said, looking at Lizzie's finger.

Lizzie pulled her finger and nothing budged. "It's sort of stuck but don't worry," she added quickly and cheerfully. "It's going to come off soon."

"Oh God . . ."

The sliding door opened and closed and Brian walked out. "Hey," he said to Mari. "How are you both feeling?" He'd gone out a little while ago and now he was standing there with a towel around his shoulders and gym shorts, no shirt. He was wet—and it didn't look, by the sneakers and socks, that he'd gone to the pool or beach.

"Were you exercising?"

"You look disgusted," he said and lifted his arm to smell himself.

"Eww," Lizzie said.

"Eww, my ass. Little Brian Anderson, you've got abs!"

"Hey, aren't you getting married?" Lizzie said.

"Yeah, but I'm not blind," Mari said. "By the way, I wanted to tell you that you can skip out on the wedding stuff, if you want. I know dinner is on the wedding itinerary but I totally get it, if you want to bail. No hard feelings at all. Having Jason here is weird, plus, it's kinda freaking Demi out, even if she doesn't say it."

"Really?" Lizzie asked.

"Sweet and sassy Demi is a jealous fool. Anyway, you come to the activities if you want to but feel free to skip some. Just make sure you're at the wedding!"

Mari and Lizzie hugged and then Mari said goodbye to Brian.

"I went for a jog on the beach," he said, answering her earlier question.

"On purpose?"

He laughed. "I guess you're feeling better." He plucked his book from her hand and opened it to a dog-eared page.

"Are you enjoying it?"

"I am, actually."

"Feels weird whenever someone I know reads one of my books." He handed it back to her. "There's a small cocktail party hosted by my publisher tonight. Can you make it? It's at seven."

"I'm supposed to join the wedding party for dinner tonight and even if she said I can skip it, I feel guilty coming all the way to Mexico, and bailing out on the wedding stuff."

He looked dejected or maybe anxious, she couldn't be sure. Should she cancel on Mari? After all, the wedding was the reason she was in Mexico. On the other hand, she had promised to attend his events with him.

"It's cool. I get it. Tomorrow, though, I'm going to need you. This is small and Violet doesn't arrive until tomorrow."

"I have the rehearsal and rehearsal dinner tomorrow and I'm going to need you."

"One sec." He jogged inside and came back with his phone. "What's your email?"

Her brows furrowed but she told him as he typed it into his phone. A moment later her phone chimed with an incoming message.

"I created a shared calendar. Add the things you need me to attend, and I'll do the same with my events. If there's a conflict with times we'll figure something out."

"Organized. I like it."

"I actually came out here to ask how you'd feel about a couple's massage?"

"I feel like there's a catch to this," she said, as they both inputted events into their respective phones.

"There's no catch. The hotel left me a coupon for a complimentary couple's massage and looking at our combined schedule the only free time we have is the next few hours. Come on, Alonso, this will be a good icebreaker for the next forty-eight hours, which are looking to be superhectic. What do you say?"

He held out his hand and she took it and helped herself up. "I'd like that."

"Cool. I'm going to take a quick shower. Why don't you make a call and see if there's availability in the next few hours?"

"Will do." She took the coupon that he handed her and went to the landline and clicked the button labeled "Spa." It felt rather domestic to work together on something. Except during his jog, they'd been together all day. Normally having people in her space bothered her.

If she had an impulse to eat Cheetos in the middle of the day, and lick her fingers clean, she didn't want any judgment. Same with an afternoon nap or deciding to review a complex contract in the middle of the night. Brian was turning out to be a pretty good roommate. She didn't have that urge to fill in the silence with idol chitchat or push him off the balcony. He'd been right about one thing—Lizzie was talkative and always felt the need to make people at ease or fill in the uncomfortable silence. But with Brian there was no uncomfortable silence. They were just two people co-existing. Now they were two people in a fake relationship about to have a real couple's massage.

Nope, this wasn't weird at all.

Chapter Six

Brian

There was something surreal about lying on a table next to his nemesis, mostly naked, except for a few strategically placed towels. Try as he might, it was very difficult to be upset when there was someone rubbing his body vigorously in an effort to expel all his stress. But there was something happening to him in that moment and it had everything to do with the woman who moaned and groaned from a foot away.

"Can you stop with all that racket?" he said, surely sounding muffled from the round hole where his head was placed.

"What? Did you say something? Oh yeah . . . right there."

"I said . . . be quiet. I can't relax with all that noise."

"Oh. Sorry," she mumbled back, genuinely sounding contrite.

He felt relieved when she stopped making all those little noises and felt himself start to melt into the message. Deadlines, fake girlfriend, fake fiancée, Violet, social anxiety . . . it was all being dispelled out of his body by the five-foot-one tiny Mexican woman currently pounding her elbows on his lower back.

"Oh God, that feels so good," Lizzie said, almost yelling in ecstasy, which of course made him think of how she'd sound in bed. She moaned again and he felt himself grow hard. He couldn't very well turn around in this state. Math always shifted his mind from sex. *Three hundred and seventy-six plus seven hundred and forty equaled one thousand orgasms on his cock from Lizzie. Shit, math wasn't helping.* He changed from math to thinking about the latest YouTube video a buddy had sent him about a gross abscess in someone's foot.

She groaned out another "ohhhh . . ." and he pushed himself up. He was going to detonate without so much as a touch if she didn't shut up.

"Señor Anderson?"

Holding his towel over his erection he hopped off the tiny table, careful not to look at his fake fiancée or the masseuse he had startled. "I'm sorry," he told the masseuse.

"Anderson? Hey, what happened?"

"What does a man have to do to get some peace and quiet?"

"What crawled up your ass?" she said and he heard

shuffling behind him as he turned out of the room and into the private changing room, slamming the door shut behind him. He needed to change into his clothes and get the hell out of there, but he was too worked up.

Stretching his arms on the changing room counter, he closed his eyes, dropped his head down, and tried to take deep calming breaths.

"What the hell, Anderson?" Lizzie walked in without even knocking and closed the door behind her. He looked up and saw her through the mirror in front of him. She was wrapped in a towel, her hair mussed, her cheeks pink, and her skin glowing.

"I need you to leave," he rasped.

"Excuse me? Why? I'm sorry I'm chatty, but this is a huge overreaction. Plus, it's so rude to just walk out of a couple's massage."

"Lisette, leave."

She crossed her hands over her chest, haughtily.

"No. You just asked me to be nice. We have an agreement and you're being a huge dickhead for no reason. You know . . . everyone seems to think you're this reserved, reclusive, nice guy who's at home dreaming up love stories but I know the real you. The real you is an ass. For a moment I thought you'd changed but the ornery jerk is back."

He closed his eyes and inhaled. Then straightened his back and turned around.

"And if you—" she began again but then her eyes drifted

down. "Oh. Oh . . ." she whispered, her hand tightening around her towel. She had the good sense to finally shut the fuck up.

He closed the distance between them, coming right up to her face. "You don't know when to stop, do you?"

"It's perfectly normal to get an erection in that kind of situation." She pointed behind her, but her eyes wouldn't meet his gaze.

He cupped her jaw and forced her to face him. "It's not the massage."

She looked at him intensely. He was about to tell her to get the hell out before he did something stupid when her lips were suddenly on his.

It was unexpected.

It shook him.

He pulled away for half a second to get his bearings. Her eyes were wide as if she had shocked them both. But the dam had been broken and there was no way to put it back together again. And hell, he didn't want to, not right now at least.

Without a second thought, he cupped the back of her neck, pulled her close, and kissed her back. Their mouths collided in an angry crash of tongues and teeth. He wrapped his arms so tightly around her waist that her back bowed. But he continued to kiss her and she continued to kiss him back, pulling his hair hard and groaning into his mouth. He lifted her up and she instantly wrapped her legs around him while he carried her to the counter and set her down.

The towel around his waist didn't make it on the short journey and her towel had fallen below her breasts.

"Need more, Anderson."

"Shut up," he said between kisses that were now trailing down her neck. Her head fell back against the mirror and her legs parted as he continued to move down, cupping her beautiful tits with his hands. She arched into him and a noise that sounded very much like a growl came out of his mouth, surprising him. He took one of her nipples into his mouth and she pressed her heels into his ass. When he finished with one nipple, he let it go with a big suction sound, and went straight for the other one.

"Oh God, condom. Need a condom," she said.

"Fuck," he groaned. They were in a spa; he did not have a condom with him.

"No no no," she said anxiously. "I hate admitting this to you, of all people, but I haven't had sex in a while. I'm clean and I'm on the pill. Please tell me your dick isn't green from all the groupie sex," she added, sounding desperate.

"I'm clean," he said, temporarily ignoring her digs about his sex life.

"Okay. Good."

He pulled her towel away and tossed it over his shoulder. He wanted to ram his cock into her but she took his breath away, sitting there completely naked for him. She was so goddamn beautiful.

"What's wrong? Why are you stopping?"

"Are you sure you want to do this?"

"Don't you?" she asked, wide-eyed, confused, and breathless.

"More than anything. I just can't believe I'm about to fuck Lisette Alonso."

"Well, if you don't hurry up, you're not," she said and reached forward, grabbed his shoulders, and pulled him toward her, kissing the hell out of him. He slid one arm around her waist and with his other hand, he positioned his cock at her entrance and pushed forward while she arched and moaned into his mouth.

Turned out, Lizzie's sex moans and Lizzie's massage moans were different. This moan made her entire body contract and reverberate against him. She wrapped her legs around him even more tightly and fisted his hair as he pistoned into her, nipping and kissing her neck.

"Don't stop, please, don't stop."

"Baby, I couldn't stop even if I wanted," he said against her neck as her pussy tightened around him almost to the point of pain. "Unless you ask me to stop. Do you want me to stop?"

He looked at her in panic.

"Hell no! Read the room, Anderson."

He chuckled and continued to push in and out of her as the need to release was almost painful. He felt when she came, her nails digging into his shoulder almost painfully as her pussy tightened around him in a vise grip. He pushed once, twice, and a third time and finally released his own intense orgasm.

Jesus Christ . . . It turned out that Lisette Alonso had made his cock fall in love with her after all. He hoped his heart would not do the same.

Lizzie

*W*hat. In. The. Actual. Fuck had just happened.

For minutes they stayed joined, his face still against her neck, his dick twitching inside of her. Both of them were breathing heavily against one another, both covered in oils from the massage and the sweat from the extracurricular sex session. She felt like Jell-O, her limbs loose and limp. Added to that was the emotional toll having sex with Brian Anderson was going to take.

Then, she came to her senses and remembered where they were.

She broke the silence first.

"Were we loud?"

"Yes."

She whimpered. "You could have lied, you know," she said as he finally pulled out of her. She quickly pressed her thighs together and slid off the counter. He wasn't looking at her as he found their towels on the floor.

Why had she kissed him?

He handed her a towel and then turned on the shower and jumped in, cleaning himself off. Quickly, she used the towel to clean herself and then grabbed another towel and wrapped it around herself. "I cannot go outside and look those women in the eyes."

"It's fine. These things happen during couples' massages. Why do you think it's a private room with a private bathroom?" he asked.

"It might be fine for you but it's not for me." She was panicking. She went to the locker and took out her clothes and started putting them on. Her hands shook. It was the adrenaline and the surprise of what had just happened. Warm hands stopped her.

"It's going to be fine, Lizzie. Trust me."

"Trust you? Yesterday you hated me and now you want me to trust you?"

"I never hated you."

She crossed her arms over her chest, a brow raised high on her face.

"Okay, I didn't like you very much but things change. Turns out, you're not so bad," he said with a smirk.

She rolled her eyes and then covered her face with her hands. He surprised the hell out of her when he brought her into his chest and hugged her. "Look, people think we're engaged. Engaged people have sex."

"In spa changing rooms?"

"Absolutely. After a couple's massage! Probably a super-popular place to have sex, actually. They're not in the other room just waiting on us to finish. They discreetly left, I'm sure." He kissed the top of her head. He released her and went to retrieve his own clothes while she did her best to fix her "just had sex in the bathroom" hair.

Once he was dressed he turned back to her. "We'll just walk out and go straight to the room."

Her heart was beating rapidly. "Fine."

She opened the door to the massage room, which was now empty. *Thank you, Jesus.* He took her hand in his and crossed the room to the door that led into the spa reception area. When he opened it, they both crashed into Pablo, who was standing in front of it like a sentry.

"Señor, señorita . . . no need to worry. I will escort you to your room through the service elevator. Follow me." He clapped twice. "Vamos. Hurry."

Lizzie and Brian looked at each other, both surprised and impressed. As if they were two dignitaries being escorted into a top secret location, Pablo led them down stairs and winding corridors. Lizzie walked with her head down the entire time, wishing her hair were longer and able to cover her face. Through a maze of halls, two kitchens, and the laundry room, they eventually made it to their villa. They'd bypassed the busiest parts of the resort.

"Gracias, Pablo. Muchas gracias." Lizzie hugged him as Brian took out the keycard and led them inside. "Do I even want to know how you knew we were there?"

The pudgy cheerful man blushed and Lizzie waved him off. "No. Never mind. I don't want to know."

"The manservant thing has its perks," Brian said after closing the door behind them.

Once in the privacy of their villa, Lizzie turned to Brian. "That was embarrassing."

He shrugged. "You're never going to see any of these people again."

That was true.

"It's not like we had sex in the hotel lobby in front of everyone."

That was also true.

"Can we talk?" she asked.

"No," he said, going straight to the kitchen. He grabbed himself a beer and offered her one, which she declined. Instead, he poured her a glass of water as she opened and closed her mouth twice. "Let me guess . . . This was a mistake. A onetime thing. It can't happen again . . . blah blah blah. Which is why I prefer you not talk."

More or less, that was what she was going to say. But now that they were here, alone, and she could still feel the effects of the delicious orgasm, she didn't want it to be a onetime thing. She wanted to do it again. The problem was, she didn't really like him. She didn't hate him but she didn't like him and she'd never had sex with someone she actively disliked. But she really, really liked the sex and wanted more of it.

"No, that's not what I was going to say."

"I can't wait to hear this." He made himself comfortable on the sofa. "And for transparency, you should know I'm hard again." He looked down at his crotch. "You make me hard. Always have, even when I wanted to throttle you."

"I have? No, I haven't."

"You have. I always found you hot. Well, not when I was ten but when I started thinking with my dick. You drove me crazy in both the worst way and the best way."

"Didn't see that coming," she admitted. "And if we're in this honesty circle, I guess I didn't exactly find you disgusting. Physically, I mean. Your personality was spiteful but I was into that broody cool guy thing you had going on."

"I mostly liked your tits and ass," he lied, playfully.

She gave him the finger. "So you don't think it was a mistake?"

"I didn't say that. It's obviously a huge fucking mistake. I'm saying that I think we should spend the next couple of days having sex. That was good, what we just did, but there's a lot more I'd like to do."

She paced around the room. "So, we could, in theory, have sex for the next few days, which incidentally fits very well into the fiancée ruse. No strings. Just sex?"

"We could," he said, placing his legs on the floor and patting his thighs. "And we should."

It took her all of two seconds to decide that this plan was amazing.

She straddled his thighs.

"See, Anderson, talking is good."

He hadn't been lying, he was already hard.

He smelled of eucalyptus and lavender and his blue eyes

were glowing with need. She thought he'd waste no time in screwing her senseless again. Instead, he took her hand in his and opened his mouth and sucked her finger deep into his mouth. Her pussy immediately wanted him.

Then he pulled her finger out and dropped Mari's ring on her palm. It was such a hot and sexy gesture, she was temporarily blinded by lust.

"Round two," she croaked and this time it was Brian who pressed a kiss on her first.

Chapter Seven

Brian

"We're late!" Lizzie said, jumping off the bed, tripping on all the tangled sheets and clothes strewn around the room.

"What time is it?" He stretched and watched the woman gather clothes into her arms, frantically. They'd spent all afternoon getting to really know one another. He'd tasted her—finally. She sucked him off—finally. And eventually, they fucked themselves into slumber. Both naked and sleeping on opposite sides of the bed.

"I have to be dressed and at the restaurant in twenty-five minutes and you have to be at your thing in forty-five minutes. I still need to shower and get ready."

"So really, *you're* late. I'm fine."

She glared at him and he chuckled. She looked good all post-sex glowing, even if she was frazzled and frantic.

"I know a way to make things faster," he said, with a toothy grin. He jumped out of the bed and before she knew what was happening, he lifted her up and threw her over his shoulder in a fireman's carry.

"Anderson!" She giggled. Giggled! He'd made "stick up her gorgeous Cuban ass" Lisette Alonso giggle. It felt like a monumental achievement.

"If we shower together we'll save time and water and I'm all about planning and conservation."

"Baby, I can't have sex with you again. There's no time."

Baby? She'd called him "baby" and it had been absent-mindedly, in a sweet, non-sarcastic way. Mostly, he'd always been Anderson or "asshole." This change disconcerted him. He cleared his throat before setting her down and turning on the shower. "No sex. Just a shower. Promise."

She didn't seem convinced, and he knew it was probably because his nether regions had started to take over at the sight of her nakedness. He ignored the way she looked at him, disbelieving anything he was suggesting. "Ignore that," he said, pushing her chin up with his forefinger to meet his gaze. "Here's the plan. I'll walk you to your dinner," he said, lathering her hair with shampoo. "I'll stay for a drink. Then I'll go to my thing."

"Are you washing my hair? This feels very . . . not fake."

"We've crossed so many lines, what damage can hair washing do?" He reached over her and took the bar of soap and dropped it on her hand. "Here, make yourself useful."

She shrugged and then started to lather him. It was both

very intimate and also strangely normal, as if they did this every day. He lathered up his own hair next and then used the handheld nozzle to remove the shampoo from her hair, followed by his.

"You don't have to come with me. It was short notice and you have your own thing."

"It's fine. I don't mind," he said. "That way the ex can see that you're taken." For some reason he wanted the ex to know this information. Even if temporarily, she was taken, and the ex needed to move along and any thoughts of a reconciliation needed to vanish from his mind.

They finished and he turned off the shower as they stepped out together and towel dried.

She went to her room, and he went back to his to dress. He appreciated the need to not have to make small talk. There was a comfortable silence between them that he really liked.

He was walking out of his room at the same time she stepped out of hers. The woman took his breath away. She wore a long dress with big yellow and red hibiscus flowers on it, paired with heels. She didn't wear a ton of makeup, which he appreciated, and the pièce de résistance was a matching red flower pinned on one side of her hair, which was tucked behind her ear.

"I like the short hair." He hadn't said that to her before but he felt the need to tell her now. He'd seen her naked, been inside of her, tasted her; the least he could do was make sure she knew he found her beautiful.

She touched it as if forgetting the length. She used to have long hair that she wore in braids or a ponytail, which he used to pull all the time. "Thanks. I did it just so that you didn't have anything to pull anymore," she said jokingly.

"I was just remembering that," he admitted. "We were kids back then. I get that I was a pain in the ass but you can't really be mad about stupid kid shit," he added.

He was struggling to tie a baby-blue tie and she instinctively pushed his hand aside and finished it as she said, "I'm not mad, per se. I just don't like you. Well, you're sort of redeeming yourself with the sex but before I saw you again, you were just someone who I would have rather never seen again."

He appreciated her honesty. It wasn't as if she'd been his first choice to run into at their reunion.

"But don't you think maybe you overreacted a bit?" he asked, immediately regretting it. They were in a good place; why was he picking this moment to rehash fifteen years of bad blood? "Never mind. Forget I said anything."

She yanked at his tie, hard.

"Hey!"

"No, you can't start something like that and then say never mind! You embarrassed me repeatedly, scared all my high school boyfriends and ruined all my Valentine's Days until I was eighteen years old. Sorry if I have a hard time seeing past that. I think I'm doing a pretty good job at it, considering all the sex we've just had."

His mouth was wide. "I did not do any of that. Maybe I yanked your ponytail a time or two—"

"Put lizards in my locker."

He tried to hold down a smile. "Okay I did do that, but I was a kid."

"You weren't a kid when you asked me out to prom and then stood me up!" she yelled.

"That never happened!"

She waved her hand dismissively. "Forget it. It doesn't really matter."

He grabbed her arm to stop her. "It obviously does because you are still mad about it."

She didn't respond; she looked mad but also hurt somehow, as if the memory of it pained her anew. He didn't like that.

"Lisette, I did not stand you up for prom."

"Are you telling me that I did go to prom, because I know for an absolute fact I did not."

"No. What I'm saying is that I did not stand you up because I never asked you to prom. Why would I ask you to prom? We hated each other."

"We chatted on AOL one night for hours and you asked me to prom."

"I never chatted with you on AOL. I didn't even have a computer at home."

Her eyes widened.

"You did. You apologized for being a dick, told me that

you always liked me, and that you wanted to ask me to prom but were too shy to do it in person."

"I wouldn't have apologized for being a dick because you were kind of a dick too and I wouldn't have asked you in a computer chat."

"Oh my God," she said, realizing that he wasn't lying and that all this anger she'd held on to for all this time had been directed at the wrong person.

"I'm sorry, Lizzie. It wasn't me. It was probably Roly Polinski or maybe Karen Da Silva."

"Son of a bitch," she said. "That was cruel."

"It was." He pulled her into his arms, and she let him.

"I never even understood why they didn't like me. What did I ever do to them?"

"You were smartest in the class, which pissed off Roly for no good reason because unlike me, he wasn't in the running to being valedictorian, nor did your A affect his F in any way. And Karen, well, you were always kinda hot and she was just a mean girl and mean girls don't like competition."

"That was not a good time. Glad high school's over," she said.

"Wait," he said and pushed her back slightly so he could look into her eyes. "You said yes."

"Pardon?"

"You were going to go with me to prom. Well, it wasn't me, but you thought it was me and you said yes. You didn't hate me."

She shoved him playfully and said, "Pfft."

He grabbed her by the wrist. "You liked me, Lisette. Admit it."

She looked into his eyes, refusing to admit defeat.

So he decided to go first. "Well, I can admit that I didn't hate you. I thought you were annoyingly beautiful and irritatingly smart and totally out of my league. It would never have even occurred to me to ask you to prom."

She stared at him for a while and he could see years of anger fizzing out little by little. "We have to go," she said.

"This conversation isn't over," he said, because he'd never put a lot of thought into why Lisette Alonso despised him and now that he knew it was a misunderstanding, he wanted—no, needed—to get to know her.

"Fine. Later." She grabbed her purse. "I can meet you at your thing when dinner is over."

"No. I'm walking you to your dinner, I'll stay for a drink. Then you can meet me at my event if you have time. Although, my thing should be quick. I can handle it on my own if you don't make it on time."

"Fine," she said. "Wait . . . you're wearing that? You look like a librarian. Not that there's anything wrong with librarians, but it doesn't seem like you."

"We've been talking for ten minutes. You tied the tie and you're telling me this now?"

She scrunched her nose, adorably. "Sorry. Was on autopilot."

"Either way, you don't even really know me and my style. I'm sure this is fine."

"Maybe you're right." She shrugged. "But you look uncomfortable. Aren't you like into building stuff? Isn't that your thing when you're not writing?"

"You googled me, how sweet."

She rolled her eyes. "We're engaged. I needed to know some things about you just in case someone asked." She waved her hand dismissively. "Anyway, you're not a suit-and-tie kinda guy, I didn't think."

She was right. He could wear a suit, but a tie . . . nope. He wasn't a tie guy. He was a "Pink Floyd T-shirt and jeans" kinda man. If the occasion called for dressing up, he was a "button-down, sleeves pulled up" type of guy.

Fuck.

He pulled the knot out of the tie and tossed it behind him.

"Brian!" she yelped. "What happened to the tie and . . ." She looked at him quizzically. "And why are you stripping? I'm not . . . what the hell are you doing?"

He chuckled. "I'm changing." He padded to his room. "You're right, I need to be comfortable. This isn't me."

"Oh. Okay. But hurry up."

"How did you get ready so fast? Women take forever."

"I'm not like every other woman, I suppose."

She was right about that. Five minutes later he came out in a checkered, less formal button shirt, sans tie, and grabbed his keys and wallet and took her hand in his. "Ready. Let's go."

THE VALENTINE'S *Hate*   139

"Uh . . . what are you doing?" She looked down at their joined hands.

He'd done it because . . . well, because it felt good to hold her hand. He wanted to do it. But they were for real fucking and pretend dating. Holding hands wasn't in the deal. But he had already done it so he said, "We haven't been seen together enough and we have to go through the lobby and two bars to get to your restaurant. If I'm with you, people won't be as quick to approach me."

It was a lie but she didn't argue about it. And that's how they walked into Las Enchiladas restaurant to meet her friends.

"OVER HERE!" MARI waved from across the restaurant the moment they stepped inside. Lizzie's grip tightened on Brian's hand. He knew why. At the table with Mari and Gus was another couple who seemed really, really into each other by the way her face was tucked into his neck; almost a bit too much for a public space.

"Hey man," Gus said, standing up and extending a hand to Brian, which he took and firmly shook. "Good to see you again."

"Sorry we're late," Brian said and then gave Mari a kiss on the cheek. Lizzie did the same, but she whispered something to Mari and then Mari was sliding her ring onto her finger.

"No worries!" Mari said. "Glad you guys made it."

"Brian Anderson, this is Demi, Gus's sister, and that's Jason, Demi's boyfriend. Jason, Demi, this is Lizzie's . . ." She hesitated for a moment, looking for the right word. "Lizzie's date."

"Nice to meet you both," Brian said.

"Sit. Sit," Gus said. "Drinks?"

"I actually have to run to a cocktail party—" he began but Lizzie wasn't releasing her grip so he pulled out her chair and then one for himself. "One drink and then I have to run. I apologize. I have a mixer thing with my publisher."

"So it is true. You are B. Anderson. Oh. My. God. I have to live Insta this!" Demi took out her phone.

Damn it.

"Uh . . . please, no no," Lizzie quickly said, waving her hand to stop Demi. "Anders . . . Brian doesn't really like to be the center of attention. How about later?" She was flustered but he really appreciated how she'd de-escalated that.

Best fake fiancée ever.

He would have hated to have been recorded while he was trying to gauge the situation between Lizzie and Jason. She turned her attention to him once Gus took his sister's phone from her hand and placed it on the table. Brian liked the man. "Let's get you a drink, sweetie, before you have to run," Lizzie said. They needed to work on their nicknames. She said "sweetie" like she'd been chewing nails and Mari had caught it because she was pressing her lips together, holding in a laugh. Brian wondered whether Mari had told Gus the truth about their fake relationship.

"So how did you two meet?" Jason asked, his arm slung around Demi. The guy had a man bun and a beard—he hated man buns and decided the next new character in his book would have a man bun and then he'd immediately have him plummet to his death from a sudden sinkhole.

"Funny story," Lizzie said. "Isn't it a funny story, sweet pea?"

"Yes, hilarious story, pumpkin. Why don't you tell it?"

They were both fresh out of stories and before the silence became too obviously weird, Mari cut in. "We've all known each other since grade school."

"How's that a funny story?" Demi asked.

"They hated each other," Mari added.

"We were neighbors," Lizzie said.

"And in the same class," Brian said.

"Brian was always playing pranks on Lizzie and generally trying to make her life a living hell."

"No, I was not." Mari and Lizzie both glared at him. Maybe he hadn't been as bad as Lizzie thought but that hadn't always been the case. In elementary school he'd been as bad as she remembered; he grew a conscience later. "Okay, fine. I wasn't great but I outgrew that around fourteen."

Lizzie's head turned to him. "But you kept messing with me well into senior year of high school. Remember when you put lizards in my locker because everyone was calling me Lizzie the Lizard?"

"Again, kid shit. That was maybe middle school if not elementary. But if we're being honest," he said, expanding on the earlier conversation that they'd had in his room, "she was always trying to one-up me. If I got straight A's she would do extra credit to get that tiny little edge over me, bumping me out of top of the class." He straightened his glasses and smiled at her, daring her to deny it. She was a competitive little witch who did her best to make him look like second fiddle all the time.

"The lizard fiasco was high school. Trust me, I vividly remember." She shivered as if the lizards were currently crawling on her. "And me getting better grades than you wasn't to compete with you. I just got better grades. I didn't do that to purposely irritate you." Her tone wasn't playful anymore and Jason's eyes were ping-ponging between them, analyzing everything.

Brian put his arm over the top of her chair and moved in closer. "Sure you didn't, lovebug."

She glared, her eyes narrowing on him.

"He ruined all her Valentine's Days," Mari added.

"Not all of them."

"Oh, buttercup, you ruined every. Single. One," she said through clenched teeth and a fake-ass smile. If Jason and Demi were buying any of this, they were dumber than a box of crayons because even with a truce between them, it was obvious they couldn't go ten minutes without challenging one another.

There was awkward silence.

"But anywho . . ." Mari said cheerily. "They reconnected

a few months ago and it looks like all that pent-up hate was just hot flaming foreplay."

"Oh . . . I love an enemy-to-lovers trope," Demi said as if she were watching a movie, her chin resting on her palm.

Lizzie and Brian smiled just as the waiter opened a bottle of wine and poured everyone a glass. It couldn't come soon enough.

Lizzie

Jason kept looking at her from across the table and it made her uncomfortable. She knew him too intimately. She knew his quirks and how he had this need to dissect every little detail of every single situation. He may have tried to give off the surfer-dude, laid-back effect, but the guy was a civil engineer who analyzed and overanalyzed everything. He wasn't one to let things go; he had to keep at it until the problem, which wasn't a problem in the first place, became a big fat dramatic argument. He was like someone with a tiny piece of cuticle on his thumb that he kept biting and pulling until it became infected and throbbed. It would have fixed itself had he left it alone. Except that, she'd learned from the years since they'd broken up, leaving things alone and hoping they'd fix themselves wasn't always the solution. There had to be a happy medium between Jason's incessant nit-picking and Lizzie's great ability to hide her head in the sand.

"You want to hear a cute story," Mari said to Demi. "He was her first kiss."

Lizzie had been mid-sip and choked on her wine when Mari spoke. Brian tapped her on her back. "You okay, baby?"

She coughed and then opened her eyes wide on her ex–best friend.

"I'm fine," she croaked out and wiped her eyes.

"That is so sweet!" Demi said. "Isn't that sweet, Jason?"

Jason took a sip of his own wine and nodded, looking at Lizzie over the rim of the glass.

"How did it happen? You guys dated before? I thought you hated each other."

"They had been playing spin the bottle and it had landed on the two of them."

"Jeez, Mariana. You're full of old stories tonight, aren't you," Lizzie said.

"What can I say . . . I love love," Mari chirped.

"Oh, me too," Demi said, clasping her hands together. "This would be the best Insta story ever." She eyed her phone on the middle of the table and Gus slid it farther away.

"It was silly. It was at a party. Tenth grade," Lizzie said.

"Ninth," Brian corrected her, and she turned to look at

him. He remembered? He'd kissed half the school by then; she knew it hadn't meant anything to him.

Jason finished off his glass of wine and took the bottle and refilled it.

"Don't you need to go?" Lizzie looked at the time on her phone. "You're already a little late."

"I'll leave shortly," he said. "I'm really enjoying all this conversation."

She glared at him some more. Thankfully, they were interrupted by a loud familiar voice from behind them. "Look who it is!"

Brian

Jason had not taken his eyes off Lizzie all night. Brian wondered if she realized the fucker was still into her. Would she be into him too? And just the fact that he was wondering that made him mad. He shouldn't care. This was all fake, after all.

"Mom, Dad, Maria, Ramon, what are you guys doing here? We thought you were going to stay in the other hotel for dinner tonight," Gus said.

"We decided to grab dinner over here. The other hotel doesn't have a great selection," one of the women said.

"Mom, you should've called. We would've gotten a bigger table," Mari said.

"Oh, hush. It's fine."

Mari introduced everyone.

"You didn't mention a date when I saw you yesterday," Maria said to Lizzie.

"He had to work, must've slipped my mind."

"And why didn't I know about this young man during our calls?" Maria asked.

"Um . . ." Lizzie began to straighten the silverware on the table and fidget with the cloth napkin. "It's new and I didn't want to jinx it."

"Have you always been superstitious?" Ramon asked. "Telling us wouldn't have jinxed it. That's silly. You know Maria loves to hear all about you girls' love lives," he said, looking at her and Mari.

"So how does this long-distance thing work? You visit her or vice versa?"

"Stop with the inquisition, Mom," Mari said just as the waiter walked by to refill the water glasses for the table.

"If you want to go, I totally understand. My mom can be relentless," Mari whispered when Maria was looking elsewhere.

"I think I'm going to head out. I'm so sorry," Lizzie whispered in return. She pushed her chair back, surprising Brian. "Look, there's a table right there for two; why don't you guys slide that table over and take our chairs."

"No, we couldn't," Gus's father said.

"No, it's quite all right. Brian has an event on the other side of the hotel. We're actually already late."

"We hate to impose," Mari's mother said.

"I'm sorry," Lizzie whispered again to Mari, who winked back in understanding.

She turned to the two older couples. "Really, it's fine. We were about to leave anyway."

"You scared her off, Maria," Ramon said.

"No. No. Really, we were going to go anyway. We'll catch up later, promise."

"It was nice meeting you all," Brian said. "Enjoy your evening."

Brian didn't know what had caused Lizzie to change her plans but he welcomed it. The more time he spent with her, the more time he wanted with her. Turned out, she was funny, thoughtful, and smart.

"What happened? You didn't have to come with me. I'll be okay," he said once they were out of the restaurant.

"I know, but it's one thing to lie to strangers and another to lie to Maria and Ramon. She was like a second mom to me growing up. She FaceTimes me almost as often as Mari. I just couldn't sit next to her through a dinner and lie to her face about us."

"So, I have a question for you about this charade," he said. "Are you doing it to make Jason jealous in the hopes he'll see what he's missing and come running back or is it because you're embarrassed that you're dateless and he's not?"

Lizzie was competitive as hell and he had assumed she wanted to one-up her ex by having a date of her own—a successful one made it a bonus. But the way Jason was looking at her, the man wanted her back, and Brian wasn't sure if he liked how that made him feel. He didn't want any part in them getting back together.

"Does it matter?" she asked.

"Yes," he deadpanned.

She looked at him quizzically. "I guess a little of both, more of the latter, though. I don't want him to come running back, although it would be good for the ol' ego if he feels jealous. I wouldn't exactly mind."

"And if he came back to you. You would take him back?"

"Hell no. Once a cheat, always a cheat. Why do you ask?"

"Because he wants you back."

She stopped walking and turned to him. "He does not. He's with Demi, beautiful bubbly Demi. They were practically dry-humping when we walked in."

"He was ogling you all night. And she was humping him; he looked bored as hell."

Her brows furrowed. She legitimately hadn't noticed when it had been so obvious to Brian. She did not know the effect she had on people—women and men. There were people that walked into the room and changed the energy. That was Lizzie, always had been. People gravitated to her. She could hold a conversation with anyone where it didn't feel forced or stilted. Yes, she was beautiful, but even if she weren't, she'd still be the most charismatic and dynamic person in the room. And her laugh . . . it was infectious. She laughed loudly and earnestly. It came from deep inside and it wasn't exactly pretty. It was honest and open. So, yes, Jason was mesmerized by the force that was Lisette Alonso, as was Brian Anderson, it seemed.

"Rein in the crazy, Anderson. Jason was scrutinizing our relationship, wondering why I hadn't mentioned the spin the bottle game while we were dating. Hell, he was wondering why I hadn't mentioned you at all while we dated," she said. "Anyway, is this where your thing is at?" She pointed to a salon where people were lounging with drinks in hand.

"Yep."

"What can I expect? Who'll be here? Anything I should know?"

"Just industry people. The heads of my publishing company, probably some of the supporting actors, executives of the studio. There may also be other authors too who have upcoming movie deals with the studio. They'll probably talk about their own books, so bonus if you've read any."

"Okkkkay. Well, let's do this thing." She grabbed his hand, and together they walked in.

As expected, there were big known authors in attendance, one huge Latin American actress, a director, some actors from Brian's movie who he'd met during filming, and some other people he didn't recognize. Brian led them to the bar and ordered himself a beer and Lizzie a merlot.

Someone accidentally bumped into her and within five minutes Lizzie knew that the woman was a romance author with over twenty successful novels and was currently shooting the second season of a very popular series nearby. She too wrote under a pen name, currently lived in London, apparently three blocks from Lizzie's flat, had three kids and an ex-husband, and loved going on book tours. They cackled over something silly before Lizzie looked back. "Oh, uh, Brian, have you met Susana?"

"Not officially, no. But I am familiar with your novels," he said, extending a hand. He wasn't a romance reader but he'd have to be living under a rock to not know Susana Grey.

"Susana, this is my fiancé, Brian Anderson."

"Shut the front door! My children are obsessed with you. That's why I'm here. Finally, the elusive B. Anderson in the flesh," Susana said. "Congratulations on all your success."

"Thank you. I'm kind of new to all of this."

"It can be overwhelming but it can also feel like a family when you start to get to know some other industry people."

Susana took out her phone. "I hate when people do this but would you mind if we took a selfie so I can send it to my kids?"

"Sure," he said, and put his drink down.

"I can take it for you," Lizzie offered.

"So is she your wild card?" Susana asked.

"I hope so, Susana," he said, and Lizzie looked at them quizzically. His face reddened a little because it didn't feel that fake at the moment.

"'Susie,' please, as I already told Lizzie." Yes, THE Susana Grey was now on a nickname basis with Lizzie. It had taken all of ten minutes. They hadn't even finished their first drink.

By the end of the evening, Lizzie had met every single person in the room. Granted there were only about twenty-five people at the event, but there'd been no way in hell Brian would have talked to more than two or three if he'd been there alone. He knew most of the actors and the producers and certainly the director, but had maybe exchanged ten words with them before today. She, on the other hand, exchanged numbers and social media handles with most of the people there.

Even if his agent, Louise, would have attended with him, it wouldn't have been half as successful of a night as it had been with Lizzie at his side. Louise may have known most of the people in the industry and could definitely make introductions, which took a lot of the burden of small talk off Brian, but she could also be a bit cold. Lizzie made acquaintances who'd surely end up being friends. In fact, he heard Lizzie make plans to have lunch with Susie in London next month.

"You are amazing," he said, taking her hand in his when they walked out. "I mean, you took a selfie with Alberto Allende. He has written over forty novels."

"I didn't do anything but talk."

"Not everyone can do that, you know. I wouldn't have known how to even break the ice and you spoke to everyone without it being awkward or feeling forced."

"Big famous author or not, it's still work, no matter how fancy of a job it is. I figured they'd have complaints just like the rest of us and once you find common ground, it's really not that difficult to open a line of communication. Sales and deadlines, I can relate, even if our product is different. Finding common ground is the best icebreaker."

"It's a gift."

"A compliment from you . . . that's a first."

"Liar." He moved in closer as they strolled slowly through the resort, hand in hand. "I'm a hundred percent sure I complimented your perfect breasts today, I know for a fact my cock paid homage to your pussy, and kissing you—"

Growing flustered, she covered his mouth with her hand. "Okay, Mr. Wordsmith. Jeez."

"Ahhh . . . I guess dirty talk is where your talent for talking stops."

"Apparently," she said, and he noticed she touched her cheeks with the back of her hand. "It's really hot in here all of a sudden."

He chuckled.

"What does 'wild card' mean? I saw it's how you sign your books and then Susana said it too."

It felt vulnerable to say it out loud for some dumb reason. "If you read your fiancé's book you'd know."

"Come on, tell me."

"I'd rather talk more about this first kiss deal that Mari mentioned. I very much remember you dating some kid around that time."

"Roger Gonzalez. He had braces and he wanted to kiss me but I was terrified of those metal brackets around my lips and tongue."

"Poor Roger. I'm honored to have been your first kiss," he said, placing a hand on his chest.

"Don't be cocky. Not everyone was as sexually active as you were. That broody mysterious game you had worked on all the girls."

"Trust me, I was not sexually active. Far from it. And the broody thing wasn't a game." He didn't want to expand, but the truth was, he had been miserable and sad and lonely. Kissing Lisette Alonso had been the highlight of that year. "Things at Casa Anderson weren't exciting. I'll tell you a secret so you can stop obsessing. You were my first kiss too."

Lizzie

Wow. Well, she hadn't seen that coming. Like many things in the last few days, she hadn't really known her neighbor as well as she'd thought. She was starting to believe that a lot of what she had thought about him was based on her assumptions and not reality.

"I'm not obsessing over anything. That was a hundred years ago."

"You're obsessing because you're the most competitive person I know and you hate the thought that I'd one-upped you by having kissed someone else first. You are ridiculously relieved even if it's been almost twenty years."

He was so right. Not that she'd admit that to anyone. Ever.

"Weren't you going steady with Cindy Mancini earlier that year? And how about Lisa Something-or-other?"

"Nah. Those were rumors someone made up."

Interesting.

They reached their villa, and he held the door open. She walked in and he went straight to the fridge and took out a beer for each of them. Lizzie hadn't wanted to sit through a dinner with Jason any more than she wanted a hole in her head. But, having Brian there had made things easier. In fact, she'd almost forgotten Jason was there at one point. The night had turned out better than she'd anticipated.

"There's a nice bottle of wine my agent sent over. It's a pinot noir; you want a glass instead?"

"Maybe after the beer," she said and tossed her shoes to a corner and plopped down on the couch. He brought her a glass and sat beside her. She tucked her feet under herself and he bent one foot up and shifted so that they were face-to-face. "I want to know more. I think I didn't know as much about you as I thought I did."

"Same," he said.

"Okay, so tell me: How was it living with your grandparents? Moving from Boston to Miami? New school, new friends?"

"How have you not run out of words yet?"

She laughed and playfully shoved his shoulder. "Why did you put lizards in my locker? That was messed up, even for you."

"Because you hated lizards and because I had spent all of winter break studying for that math test and you were the only one that got an A, and the fact you scored so high fucked up the curve for everyone. You're lucky you only got a few lizards. The class wanted to throw you into the canal by the school."

"Har-har."

"No, I'm serious. I overheard a few kids talking about you and whether you knew how to swim. They were going to push you into that gross canal, so I got them to agree to the lizard thing. So anyway . . . you're welcome."

"So you're trying to tell me that you did me a favor by putting lizards, which are the things I am most scared of, into my locker."

"That canal is disgusting, so yes."

She rolled her eyes. "It was a dick move, Anderson."

"I see we're back to 'Anderson.' Personally, I preferred 'snookums,'" he said playfully. "I got suspended for two days for that, by the way. Apparently the administration frowns upon lizards in lockers. So not only did I not get an A on the test, I also got in deep shit with my grandparents."

Brian got a distant look on his face, almost like regret, and she wasn't sure if she should pry. It wasn't her place.

Delicately she asked or rather commented on something he'd said earlier, hoping he would expand on it. "You said your grandparents wouldn't have accepted you being an author and now it seems as if grades and being good were very important to them. But I lived next to you guys for years and I never got that impression of them. Hell, during college, I had Sunday dinner with them a few times. They were never anything but proud of you. And they weren't strict, I don't think. Not like my mom was."

Brian took a big pull of his beer and reached for her hair and twirled it in his fingers. "Grades were very important to my parents. Had they been alive they would have been strict and disappointed had I not done well in school. I knew this for a fact. But more than that, my elderly grandparents suddenly had a kid to raise. Their time raising children had come and gone and now they had me. I wanted to make sure that I was no trouble. I wanted to be the best kid I could be. The last thing I wanted to do was be a burden on them. I didn't want to make their lives more difficult. Good grades, good behavior, a scholarship, and out of their hair. In my mind, that was what had to happen."

Lizzie watched his eyes as he absentmindedly tangled his fingers in her hair. He obviously didn't love the topic of his past, specifically of his grandparents. She wished she'd known about his relationship with them back then; it would have made her see him completely different. Now, as an adult, it all made sense. She suddenly felt bad for think-ing he was a rebellious jerk back then when he was just try-ing his absolute hardest to be perfect for his grandparents. "I'm sorry, Brian. You were dealt a shitty hand growing up and I should have been more of a friend and less of a rival."

He shrugged. "You were a kid. How would you have known? Plus, you probably had your own shit going on. Your mom was always working."

"I had my abuela, though. She was the best."

"She was pretty awesome, so was your mom."

"So were your grandparents, Brian."

He shrugged again. "They were. Taking on a kid wasn't easy, I'm sure."

"And they lost their daughter, just like you lost your mom."

"Yeah, I know. Some people have it worse, I shouldn't complain. At least I had them."

Lizzie nodded in agreement and then yawned.

"I'm sorry I'm boring you," he said, an eyebrow tipped high on his forehead as he drank his beer.

She chuckled, leaned in, and shoved him playfully. "Shut up. I'm tired. Not bored."

"Bed?" he asked.

"Bed," she confirmed. But he wasn't sure which bed she'd go to since they'd had a lot of sex earlier today.

She stood up, lifted her arms, and stretched with another yawn. Damn . . . he wanted her in his bed even if it was just to sleep. She reached her hand down to pull him up. It was a sweet gesture, almost like an olive branch. Any dislike they harbored for one another vanishing with this conversation. He took her hand in his and stood up. Softness, sexiness, and confidence, that was Lizzie, and he shouldn't have been surprised when she led him to his room.

His heart did a weird swirl-skip.

Something that should never happen with his fake fiancée.

Chapter Eight

Brian

They'd fallen right to sleep and he'd been more than okay with it.

However, sometime in the middle of the night, in the dark, Brian woke up with lips roaming his jaw and down to his neck. It was the best middle-of-the-night wake-up call he'd ever received. He gripped her by the waist and shifted her over him; her wet folds made him groan when he pushed up, while she slid down. No words were uttered. He couldn't even see her face but he could surely feel her undulating on him, slowly. He held on to her small waist until they both climaxed and Lizzie collapsed on his chest, where she fell back to sleep.

It was arguably the best night of his life.

Now, it was morning, and he was again holding this

woman tightly around the waist, acting as the big spoon after having moved to a more comfortable position during the night. He wasn't a cuddler, or so he'd been told. He often got hot and uncomfortable. When it was time for sleep, he literally wanted sleep. But this felt good. Too good, in fact.

She turned into his arms, and they were now face-to-face. "Ugh. Today's going to be the worst," she said.

"Why's that, baby?" He tucked a stray hair behind her ear. The word slipped from his lips. He wanted to rewind and unsay it but it was out there now, along with his feelings.

She tucked her head against his chest. "So many activities. You have lunch with your publisher, which you said you'll go to alone. I have a manicure and pedicure appointment with the women of the wedding party at the same time, more or less. Then we have your big meet-and-greet thing this evening, which is after the rehearsal and rehearsal dinner. Jam-packed day of craptivities."

"Luckily, it's all in the same hotel. I'm already fucking tired just listening to the itinerary."

"Yeah, me too. This hotel is huge and we have to do outfit changes and . . . it's just going to be a long and exhausting day."

"If you had a choice, what would you do instead?" he asked.

"Nothing. Absolutely nothing. I'd lie in bed, get room service, maybe read, maybe enjoy the beach and a few cocktails."

"Yeah," he said, rolling onto his back and taking her with him. "That actually sounds so much better."

"Do you write every day?" she asked, tracing the tattoo on his collarbone with her soft fingers.

"I write almost every day. I try to stay on a schedule but it's not like a nine-to-five situation. I set up a word count goal depending on my deadline and so long as I hit that goal every day, I'm good."

"And that takes what, a couple of hours?"

"Depends. Sometimes I'm really feeling the scene and I'll get the word count in, in an hour. Sometimes I'll find myself sitting in front of my computer for eight hours and nothing comes out, or rather, it's all mostly crap that comes out."

"And for fun? What do you do for fun?"

"I like to build furniture. I've sold some, actually. I don't do it to make money, it's just something I like to do. My granddad taught me how to do it. It keeps my hands and brain occupied. I've also found that it's the best thing to get rid of writer's block. If I change the scenery, get really into something I'm building, when I go back and sit in front of the computer again, words tend to start flowing."

"That's cool. I actually saw some of your work online."

"Oh, that's right, you googled me."

She playfully smacked his chest.

"How about you? You work at Dunberry, right?"

"I guess you googled me too." Her eyebrow cocked up. "Dunberry owns most of the big department stores in the malls. The last couple of years I've been in charge of all mergers and acquisitions. I'm the one that goes in and makes sure that when we acquire a new store, everything merges harmoniously."

She said the last word in quotes.

"Does it always happen like that?"

She laughed. "Never. But I guess that's where my big mouth helps. I talk to the staff and figure out what is wrong. Usually, their concerns are fear driven. Most people think they'll lose their job and I developed a program for the new staff to welcome the old staff, and vice versa. After doing this for five years, I've realized that the key is communication. They used to come in, buy up a store, and not talk to anyone about it. People were left scared and confused. I don't believe in overcommunication. People are at ease when they know where they stand, even if it's bad news."

"And it took you to London."

"Yeah, we've been buying up stores all over London."

"And you like living in London?"

"I do, but I also miss the States. We're at the tail end of a merger and honestly, I don't know what I'll do next. They asked me to head their Italian division but I don't know if I want to move again. The thought of uprooting again, it's not all that exciting anymore."

"And when is that happening?"

"I'll stay on board for a month or two to see that this last transition is smooth and then I might be done," she said, twirling the small splay of his chest hair in her fingers.

"What happens if you don't take the Italian offer?"

"For the first time in my life I have no idea."

"I doubt that Lisette Alonso doesn't have a plan."

"I really don't. I've been thinking about starting a consulting firm."

His phone rang at that moment and she reached over him and grabbed it from the nightstand and handed it to him.

"Louise, how do you feel?" Brian greeted his agent.

"Better. Better. But not as good as you, it seems."

He rolled Lizzie gently off him and then sat up, his body becoming rigid, and his jaw clenched as he listened to his agent. Lizzie must've noticed the change in his demeanor, because she too sat up, holding the blanket up by her neck. Her eyes were wide, waiting for whatever it was that put him on edge.

"Care to explain?" he asked, putting the phone on the bed and pressing the speaker button.

"'B. Anderson, author of the worldwide phenomenon the Invaders series, is set to marry businesswoman Lisette Alonso in secret Mexican wedding.' That's in *Entertainment Weekly*. Another one, this one from TMZ, says, 'Secret wedding, secret baby, Gwinnie and Zeth creator, B. Anderson, shotgun wedding to mystery woman.'"

Brian pinched his nose with this thumb and forefinger and Lizzie plopped back down on the pillow. "Shit," she whispered.

"I leave you alone for three days . . ."

"It's not like that, we're not engaged. Hell, we're not even dating. She's an old friend helping me out since you couldn't be here."

"There's always some truth to every story, Bri. You know that."

"Not in this one, Louise. Not in this one."

"Well, I don't know how you're going to get to change this narrative, not that it's terrible. Your books sales have jumped back up to the top ten in the *New York Times* Best Seller list."

"Don't worry, we have this figured out," Brian said, looking down at the woman who had her face underneath a pillow, which he plucked off her and tossed to the floor.

"Famous last words," Louise said. "Heads up, Violet landed in Cancún three hours ago. She's not going to be happy with this news."

"I could give a fuck what Violet thinks."

"We talked about this, Bri. You can't be too aggressive with her. She'll walk out of the franchise. The studio won't shoot the next two movies if this first one flops. There's millions at stake for you. You don't have to sleep with her but . . . indulge her, at least."

Lizzie's eyes narrowed.

"Not gonna happen."

"That's what'll happen to your career if you fuck this up. I mean this with love, Bri. Be careful," she said and hung up.

"Louise seems great," Lizzie said sarcastically.

"Ignore all of it; let's get up and ready for the world's longest day."

She reached for her own phone. "Should I google us?"

He took her phone out of her hand and shook his head. "Probably not. Anyway, there's not much we can do about it at this point. Let's just go with it and then we'll stage a breakup or something."

"These things never work out, ya know? Have you not seen any rom-coms?"

He laughed and then rolled over her, his forearms on either side of her face. "Before the dramatic breakup scene there's always a sex montage. I vote for the sex montage." He winked. "Plus, there's not going to be a dramatic breakup because you and I will never have feelings for each other, right?" And before she could answer, his lips were on hers.

BRIAN GRABBED THE keycard and his wallet while Lizzie finished drying her hair. "See you here at three?" he asked from the bathroom door.

She turned off the blow-dryer and looked at him through the mirror in front of her. "Yep. Good luck with your lunch."

He wasn't sure why he did it but he planted a kiss on the crown of her head and then left. Catching feelings was the last thing he wanted but Lisette Alonso was crawling her way into his heart. On the way to the restaurant, he passed by a few fans who asked for autographs and selfies. There were a few congratulations as well, and he smiled and waved.

He gave his name to the hostess at the front of the steak house. "Yes, your party is waiting for you. Right over here."

They led him to a table with four executives he didn't recognize in person although he had spoken to them on occasion. They stood up as he reached the table and introduced themselves. James Crandon, Olivia McDougall, Chris Patrick, and Jose Mendez.

"A congratulations is in order!" Jose exclaimed.

"Oh . . . uh . . . yes. Thanks."

"Where is Ms. Alonso?" Olivia asked, making it clear they were congratulating him over the pretend engagement and not the book sales.

"She actually has a wedding at this same venue and has some pre-wedding preparations scheduled today," Brian replied.

"Well, isn't that a coincidence," Olivia said.

It was a coincidence, actually. One that made the farce even more obviously fake. But there was no way around it now. He wished they'd had discussed this more so he would be ready for questions.

He cleared his throat. "She lives in London and we were gobsmacked when we found out that both events were in this same resort. It's not often that we can travel together."

The rest of the lunch was mostly about the book, thank God. But then it started to take a turn toward Gwinnie and Zeth. He almost wished they'd focus their energy on Lizzie again.

"Have you put any thought on the Gwinnie and Zeth story line?" James said.

"We've been doing some testing and we think your readers are starting to get bored with the wait," Jose added.

"I've thought about it, yes," he said. "It's just not time yet."

"We disagree," Olivia said with a smile that was so obviously fake, it made Brian want to get up and leave.

"Well, it's my book and I don't think it's quite the right time yet."

"Fans won't stick around forever. We just want to make you become the star you deserve to be."

"With all due respect, my books are selling very, very well."

"Yes, and now we need the movie to succeed in order for the studio to buy the entire franchise. This is the time to release *the* book. *The* book, not just another book . . . the best one yet, and that means your two main characters need to get it on. People love love and they love sex. If this next book takes off it'll bring more buzz to the movie and your backlist."

Brian pierced a piece of asparagus and brought it to his mouth, chewing it slowly. He understood the point and he wasn't completely disagreeing, he just wasn't sure it was the right time for the characters.

"I'll take it into consideration," he finally said, which seemed to appease them. At least for now.

Brian was walking out of the restaurant when he saw her. If she thought she was being sly, she was nuts. The woman wore a trench coat and a very obvious red wig, as if she could possibly be anyone but Violet Gram.

"There you are," she said, sidling up to him, her hands on his chest. "I was wondering when we would run into each other."

Brian took a step back.

She took a step forward.

"Violet, people are watching. You're married."

She dropped her hands to her sides. "Villa 4e. Meet me there."

"I don't think it's a good idea."

"You don't need to think, darling. Just meet me there."

"Violet . . ."

"I just need to discuss a few things about the character, is all. I saw the script for the second movie and a few things don't make sense." She winked and walked away.

His mind raced. Lizzie was mostly what he thought about; they weren't a real item or anything and he didn't owe her any explanation but still, it felt wrong to meet Violet in her villa knowing she had zero interest in discussing the movie or any character. With this in mind he went straight to his room and decided that Violet was just a bad idea in general.

Lizzie

Lizzie and Mari had their feet soaking in warm water while Demi and the mothers were having their brows waxed in another room.

"I finally get you all to myself," Mari whispered. "What's really going on with Brian?"

"What do you mean? I told you the story."

"Yeah, you told me the story but what I saw last night at dinner didn't jive with the pretend bullshit you fed me. Girlfriend, that did not look fake to me."

"Please. Of course it was," she said dismissively. "Does Gus know?"

"Know what? That you're dating Brian? Yes, he knows. He saw it with his own two eyes."

"No! That it's pretend."

"I didn't mention it because I don't think it is. The way he took care of you, of us, at the bar didn't feel pretend. Then last night was certainly real. I'm telling you, he's into you. Big-time. And if we're being honest, so are you with him."

"Have you been sniffing the nail polish?"

"I was watching you both, and girlll . . . so was Jason. You didn't even direct your attention to him. You kept leaning toward Brian, which, by the way, was making Jason crazy, but I digress . . . you were leaning, holding hands. It was really cute."

Lizzie closed her eyes and exhaled.

"What aren't you telling me?" Mari asked.

"We slept together," she whispered. "But that doesn't mean anything," she quickly added.

"It means everything," Mari said. "I don't understand why it needs to be pretend. Maybe it started that way but it doesn't have to end that way."

"I live in London and he lives in Boston."

"That's just an excuse and you know it. You don't love London and you've been telling me you want out."

"It's Brian Anderson," Lizzie whispered a bit too loudly.

"Yeah, exactly. The boy you've been half in love with since we were little girls."

Lizzie shook her head. Being with him felt so good, so right, but it had only been a few short days.

"I don't know, Mari."

"All I'm saying is, don't shut it out. Things don't have to be over on Sunday."

"Hey! What are you two chatting about?" Demi singsonged on her way to the chair next to them, followed by the moms.

"Nothing much, just wondering about the honeymoon," Lizzie said, knowing that would completely change the focus from her to Mari.

She sat there for the next hour pretending to listen to the

women chat but really, she was thinking of the possibility of having Brian in her life past Sunday.

"ARE YOU SURE you're okay? You've been off since you got back from the spa," Brian said from his room. He was wearing a towel around his waist and his hair was still wet from the shower. He didn't have his glasses on and was squinting a bit as he spoke.

"How bad do you see without them?" she asked.

"Without my glasses? Pretty bad. You're a blurry blob right now but I do see you cleaning the kitchen and the housekeeper was here earlier and left the rooms immaculate, so you're worried about something. Don't need glasses to see that."

"You look sexy with the glasses," she said.

"And now you're deflecting." He reached forward and pulled her to him. "What's going on? Talk to me."

"There's nothing going on. I'm fine. Talk to me about your meet-and-greet tonight. What can I expect?"

"I'll probably be propped up on a stage with a table and people will make a line to have their books signed and take photos. After that, however, there's a Q-and-A session, which is what I'm dreading. I'll be on that stage alone with a mic and a room full of people. They're expecting over three hundred people." She saw the anxiety on his face as he said this. It wasn't a small affliction. It was a huge ordeal for him.

"Stage fright sucks. I can't help you get over it with a snap of my fingers. However, as someone who was in speech and debate club in high school and college, I can give you tips."

"Let me guess, picture the audience naked." Still with only his towel. Her eyes wandered to his naked torso absently. Of course he noticed.

She rolled her eyes. "I mean, it helps but no. The key is to know your material. If you know your material well then there's nothing to fear and lucky for you, you are the star; it's your book and it's sci-fi so you can make up the shit you don't know."

"Ugh . . ."

She had an idea that she thought would help but she didn't want to tell him until she was able to see if it was doable.

"I need to answer a few emails," she said.

"Now?" he asked, surprised at her abrupt change of subject.

"Yep." She turned and went to her room, closing the door behind her. She called the front desk and asked for Pablo's number.

"Buenos tardes, Pablo," she said. "This is Lizzie."

"Good afternoon, Señorita Lizzie."

"I'm calling because I need some help with something and I think you may be able to help," she whispered.

"Of course, anything," he said.

"You may not know this but Brian has a little stage fright and tonight is a big night for him. I think a way to make him feel a little more at ease would be, instead of propping a microphone in the middle of the stage where he's the center of attention, if he were sitting at a table behind the microphone, and maybe I can sit with him, also maybe his publisher. You can put some water on the table and snacks. I don't know. Something less formal."

"I can speak with the crew preparing everything. That is not a problem," he said in Spanish.

"Muchas gracias, Pablo."

"It's my pleasure, señorita"

She felt better about this. This would make things easier.

There were a few unanswered emails from William. She'd gone most of the day without checking her emails, which was uncharacteristic of her. She quickly read them and answered. There were also notifications from social media where she'd been tagged. She tried to ignore them but it was difficult. Mostly the posts were speculation about why she and Brian were engaged. Who was Lizzie, the woman who'd nabbed B. Anderson? Of course, this led to a social media rabbit hole and she noticed Brian was tagged in a photo: "B. Anderson and Violet Gram seen together in a compromising position amidst rumors of his engagement to another woman."

It was a photo of Brian earlier today with a woman who looked like Violet trying to disguise herself. Her hands were on his chest and it looked quite intimate. Why hadn't he mentioned it to her? Normally, she wouldn't ask because once a cheater . . .

But she didn't want to jump to conclusions since he'd told her how pushy Violet was and how much he didn't want her.

He knocked on her bedroom door. "Why is it locked? Are you sure you're okay?"

She stood and unlocked the door. "Everything's fine."

He was wearing his glasses now. Before she knew what he was up to, he lifted her and threw her on his shoulder and then dropped her on her bed, straddling her.

"You're a terrible liar," he said, bending down to kiss her neck. "Tell me."

She hesitated, enjoying the kisses; her hands were being held down by his and she wanted to touch him so badly.

"Why didn't you tell me you saw Violet today?"

He shrugged. "It was nothing and I didn't want you to overthink it."

"I wouldn't do that."

He narrowed his eyes.

"Okay, fine. Maybe I would but I'm not overreacting now. I'm literally asking you. I'm not ignoring you, packing up my shit, and never speaking to you again. I'm asking. You should have told me. I didn't like finding out from an online picture."

"Promise me something."

"What is it?"

"If you get mad at me for whatever reason, you'll talk to me. All this fame BS is new to me but so far, I'm not loving all the shit that they print and post without getting all the facts. I can see where it's easy to come to the wrong conclusion if you don't get the context of the photo or article. Also, when my ex left, she didn't do much explaining. I wish I would have pushed for more answers."

"So you want me to talk to you? You know I'm not much of a talker."

"Har-har," he said.

"We literally have one more day of this thing between us. I don't know why you'd care that much what I think," she said.

"I do care. Violet asked me to meet her in her room. I didn't go. I didn't think it was right to do that to you even if we're just pretending."

It was her turn to tell him the truth. "I don't . . . maybe it doesn't have to end on Sunday. I mean, it's fine either way but if you didn't want it to end . . . the sex is good so . . ."

He chuckled into her neck.

"It took a lot for you to admit that, I know."

"It's not an admission. It's just like an idea. It's no big deal either way."

"I like it." He kissed her neck more firmly this time, nipping a little. "I like you."

It wasn't exactly a yes, but she would take it. Except that he added, "I can't do a relationship though. You deserve romance and I'm not romantic. All my previous girlfriends have made it clear that I'm terrible at romance and have eventually been hurt by something I've done or failed to do. I don't want to hurt you but I can definitely do more of this. We don't have to be enemies, you know? We could be, I don't know, friends?" He continued kissing down her neck. What the hell did that even mean? "No more fake. Real." Kiss. Kiss. "Real fun."

I can't do a relationship. Fun.

Casual, sex, and fun. He would commit to that but not a relationship.

By the time the kisses reached her belly button she was all in for fun too.

"DO YOU THINK I can wear this for both the rehearsal thing and the meet-and-greet later?" He wore a white button shirt, no tie, and a blazer. He paired it with slacks, his hair slicked back. He looked the best she'd seen him look.

"Yes. That works."

"Okay, good. You look beautiful, by the way." *Beautiful enough to sleep with but not to be in a relationship.* She wasn't sure she wanted a relationship, but being rejected outright stung. Lizzie slid it to the back of her mind. This trip wasn't about her. It was about Mari and her special day and she wasn't going to put any more thought into Anderson.

She'd decided on a short cream-colored dress, a little tighter than she'd normally opt for, but she felt good in it. Fake or real, she wanted him to drool a little. "Thanks. Help me with this?" she asked, reaching behind her neck to try to close a thin beaded choker. He walked behind her and clamped it, his warm breath on her neck shooting goose bumps down her arms.

"All right, let's do this," he said, and she took his hand, laced her fingers into it, and they were off.

"In theory, a beach wedding is romantic and beautiful. In reality, it's messy," she said when they crossed over the cement walkway into the beach area.

"Here, I'll help you," he said, bending to his knee and helping her remove her heels. He removed his own foot-wear and placed their shoes in a rack that was put there for that exact purpose. Greetings were exchanged but it was short-lived, as the very stern and efficient wedding planner started yelling directions into a bullhorn.

"Fred missed his flight. He won't be here until tomor-row morning," Mari said in a panic. Fred was the best man. "By the way, Glenda, wedding planner."

"It's going to be fine," Lizzie said and then Gus went to her and repeated it over and over. "It's fine, baby. Don't stress. Breathe."

Mari pushed Gus away. "Don't tell me it's going to be fine. This is the smallest wedding in the history of wed-dings and one person is missing; that's like eighty percent of the guests!"

"If you count you and me, and Lizzie's date, it's about seven or eight percent," Gus, stupidly, said.

"Gus!" Mari stomped her foot in frustration. "Not the right fucking time to show off your math skills."

"Mari, he's going to be here and if he's not, I'll make sure the rings make it to the ceremony. Don't stress over this. Gus is right, it's going to be fine," Lizzie assured her.

Mari glared at both of them and then turned and walked away, clearly not "fine."

"I didn't think she'd be bridezilla," Gus whispered.

"I suggest you don't point that out," Lizzie replied and Gus pretended to zip his lips and then went back to his fiancée and apparently whispered something lovingly to her, causing her to relax.

Meanwhile, Brian went to the bar to grab himself a beer and a water bottle for Lizzie. She watched the way Gus and Mari interacted. He was sweet and understanding and didn't give her shit for her crazy. In fact, he seemed to love her brand of crazy and one day, Lizzie hoped someone would love her that way too.

Mari breathed in and out, while Gus whispered something in her ear. A moment later Jason walked to the beach, alone.

"Where's Demi?" Lizzie whispered, taking Jason's hand and pulling him to the side.

"She had a headache and stayed in the room," he said. "Not a big drinker."

"At twenty I wasn't a big drinker either," Lizzie said to her ex.

"Twenty-eight," he corrected her with a smirk and she immediately regretted making the snarky comment, realizing it had come out almost like a jealous snip. "I'm actually glad to have a moment alone with you. How have you been? You look great, Iz. Real great."

"I'm good. Excellent, actually. Mari's going to have an aneurysm if Demi doesn't show up."

"Nothing I can do about that," he said dismissively. "Maybe we can get a drink later and catch up."

"I'm good," she said with a fake smile.

"Where's Demi?" Mari asked just as Demi appeared, looking rough.

"I'm here. I'm here," she said, clasping the sides of her head.

"Oh, thank God," Mari said.

"Okay, okay. Everyone, please take your places." The wedding planner clapped loudly. "Women this way. Men this way," she said, directing them.

Lizzie turned to the wooden walkway where she'd been told to stand just as Brian walked back and took a seat in the middle of the chairs where the guests would be sitting tomorrow. "Jason, please fill in for the best man," Gus said and Jason did as instructed.

After the wedding planner yelled a number of other instructions and placed people where she wanted them, she stepped back and clapped her hands.

"Okay, good!" she said enthusiastically. "And, go!" She pointed to her assistant, who clicked on a phone and music began to pour out.

"Okay, groom, you go the moment the music begins. Slowly, this isn't a race," she said loudly. "Bridesmaid, you're next," she said to Demi. "Best man, maid of honor, you're next," she said. Lizzie took the opportunity to look at Jason, who was walking toward her. He was handsome back then and the years had been good to him. She used to fantasize about their kids. Would they be blond and tall like him? Maybe they'd get her dimples and his blue eyes. She'd been so stupid. When he reached her, he put his elbow out and she slid her arm through it and they turned toward the altar, walking slowly down to it.

"Probably should have been us, huh?" he said and she stopped and stared at him, slack-jawed.

"Why would you say that? Don't say shit like that."

"Sorry. Sorry. Can't help thinking that you were the best thing that ever happened to me and I screwed it all up."

"Yes. You did."

"Less talking, more walking, people!" Glenda yelled.

"I wish you would have called me, answered a text or something. I could've explained. It didn't have to end the way it did."

Why was he bringing all this up? She refused to meet his eye and just kept walking. Right foot together. Left foot together. Why was this aisle so fucking long!

"It ended the way it did because you screwed another woman, Jason."

"And I was so sorry. I was young and stupid and you didn't even give me a chance to explain. You are too unforgiving. It's not good for the soul."

When they reached the altar they were supposed to part and walk their separate ways but he kept his hold on her.

"Don't talk about my soul and let go of me," she said and pulled her arm away from him. When she turned around to look back, Brian was watching them. She looked down; tomorrow she'd be holding flowers. Today she just stared at her bare toes in the sand.

Two men watched her. Since this was just a rehearsal, there was nowhere for her to look other than at the two men or at her feet. She started to sweat. Glenda snapped her fingers inches from her face. "Hello, are you even listening? Here. This is where you'll stand tomorrow. You're not the bride, you need to move aside."

Her cheeks flushed.

Probably should have been us.

Why did he have to say that to her?

There were no ring bearers or flower girls. She'd want kids at her wedding. They'd lighten things up and there was nothing cuter than boys in tiny tuxedoes.

"Okay, so, everyone good? Any questions?" the wedding planner asked after Mari and her father walked up and he handed her to the groom. They went through a few specific instructions after that, but it was pretty obvious what was supposed to happen next.

"No questions? Great. Now, bride and groom go first," Glenda said. "Then maid of honor and best man." Lizzie stepped toward Jason, linked her arm around his elbow, and walked alongside him. "And then the bridesmaid."

"This is so stupid. It's like I'm an adult flower girl," Demi whined.

"You wanted to be in the wedding and you're in the wedding," Mari said through gritted teeth.

"Eleven o'clock, pool bar," Jason whispered into her ear before they parted at the end of the aisle.

She was about to say no when the wedding planner yelled, "Okay, if you all follow me, I'll walk you to the dinner area."

Lizzie turned to find Brian. He hadn't moved from where he'd been sitting. She walked over and sat beside him. "What's up? We're all headed to dinner."

"You said you weren't interested in the ex."

She furrowed her brows. "I'm not."

"You sure, because there was some intense-looking conversation happening." He turned his face toward her. "And the guy can't stop staring at you."

"You and I are just fun. We're not in a relationship." She stood up. The man had made it super clear that he didn't want a relationship, so she wasn't going to explain to him how she felt talking to Jason. The moment he'd suggested "friends," the cage around her heart went up, closed, and the keys had been tossed somewhere in the Gulf of Mexico. She held out her hand. "Come on, we have dinner and then your event to get to."

BRIAN HAD THOUGHT they were in a better place now that they'd had a chat about things past Sunday. They'd agreed that they could continue the fling or at least not quite end it. They needed to talk logistics since they lived on different continents but friends with benefits was a perfect situation for him. Maybe she'd even be willing to meet him at some of the events throughout the year that he dreaded going to.

Don't fall in love with me, she'd said.

So he'd been surprised she wanted to continue it. It was real now. Not the engagement part, but the dating part. Brian was terrible at relationships and she was a hopeless romantic. Maybe one day, if the friends with benefits worked out, they could be something more, but right now, he couldn't give her more than sex. Mostly because he didn't want to hurt her like he'd hurt Sylvie and if he committed to something more than what they had right now, he would undoubtedly fuck it up and he'd lose her forever.

But she'd been acting weird since they talked. He wondered what Jason had said to her that had made her pull back in such a big way.

He took her hand and stood. "Your water bottle," he said, handing it to her. Instead of holding his hand, something they'd been doing, she drank water and busied her hand with it.

"Are you sure you're okay?" he asked.

"Yes, of course. Everything's great."

THE REHEARSAL DINNER was interesting. An elderly woman he hadn't met before was waiting there, at the wedding party's table.

"Tía Lily!" Lizzie exclaimed. "Cómo estás?"

"Lisette. How are you?" Tía Lily said as they hugged. "Who's this young man?"

Lizzie separated from the hug. "Tía Lily, this is Brian. Brian, this is Mari's aunt."

Brian held out his hand to the woman, who seemed too frail to fly from one country to another for a wedding. There was a cane propped by the wall.

"When did you get here?" Lizzie asked.

"This morning but I had to rest a little while. I could not miss my Mari's wedding day."

"I'm so glad you're here. I haven't seen you in too long," Lizzie said.

"You've gained so much weight since I last saw you, Lisette. You look bella! And your hair is so short," she said, touching it with her small wrinkly fingers. The weight part was a compliment because Lizzie knew that the old Cuban woman found curves and meat to be the definition of beautiful. The hair was probably not a compliment because Lily hadn't complimented it, she'd merely noticed it. If it had been anyone other than Tía Lily she'd feel insulted.

"The humidity in London was weighing down my hair. I thought I would cut it."

"Ahh, bueno, it will grow," Lily said. *Definitely didn't like it.* "And this one?" she asked about Brian. "This gringo is your boyfriend?"

"He's my date to the wedding."

She eyed Lizzie with a raised brow. Not missing the fact that she hadn't acknowledged whether he was or was not her boyfriend. Lizzie couldn't lie to her. "Maria reminded me about the other one." She pointed to Jason. "Ese es más guapo."

Lizzie laughed loudly, a snort even escaping her. She covered her mouth.

"Lily, you don't have to say all your thoughts out loud," Maria said from across the table.

"Did she just say that your ex is better-looking than me?" Brian asked.

"Yes, she did," Ramon replied to Brian. Jason looked smug at the comment. *Shit, had everyone heard?* "As the kids say, you better put a ring on it soon." Apparently they hadn't seen the tabloids showing that he had already put a ring on it.

"Okay, okay," Mari said. "Change of subject. Lizzie, Brian, you are over there. Tía, you're here next to Mom. Please behave."

A moment later, they all finally sat. "That was . . . something."

"Tía Lily is something else, all right," Lizzie said, laughing into her napkin. "I need a drink."

"Me too." Brian signaled for the waiter. "Two vodka sodas with a lime, not lemon. Thanks."

The night was about Mari and Gus, who were so very loved. Their families shared stories about the couple and they kissed and smiled at one another in that way couples sometimes did. As if they were keeping a secret from the rest of the world. She wanted that. One day she'd have that.

Clearly, it wouldn't be with Brian. He'd been brutally honest about it, in fact.

Demi asked Brian repeatedly for a selfie and he finally relented and agreed to one photo and ten signed books that she could give away on her site.

"I'm sorry we have to cut it short but Brian has an event," Lizzie announced.

"It's no problem," Gus said and everyone gave them their goodbyes. Tía Lily declared, "Puede que no sea tan guapo, pero es inteligente. La belleza se desvanecen pero la inteligencia dura. Elige siempre la inteligencia o dinero. Dinero dura también!" She winked at Lizzie, who covered her mouth with her palm. The lady was too much. Everyone groaned but it was out and there was no way to unhear it.

"What did she say?" Brian asked.

"She said you're smarter than him even if you aren't as handsome. She said looks fade but intelligence doesn't. She said to always choose a smart man over a good-looking one or to choose money over either."

"Tía Lily," Brian said. "I have both, money and intelligence." Brian was a good sport. Jason didn't seem as agreeable. They walked out of the restaurant and Lizzie exhaled.

"One more to go," she said.

"It wasn't that bad, was it?"

Her feet were burning. Why had she decided on these heels? She leaned a hand on the wall and took off one shoe and rubbed her sole. "It wasn't great but it wasn't horrible. So, give me the lowdown. How are you feeling?"

"Nauseous. Sweaty. At least I'm smarter than your ex, so that makes me feel a little better, I guess."

She chuckled. "It's going to be fine. Just answer the questions. Be yourself. If you get too overwhelmed let me know and I'll make something up. If you say . . . 'margarita,' I'll know you're spiraling and I'll come save you."

"I wish you could be onstage with me," he said, and she did too. Hopefully Pablo was able to pull off their sitting together at the table

She put her shoe back on and stood straight. "Okay, I'm ready. You?"

"Nope. But let's do it anyway."

Chapter Nine

Lizzie

To say Lizzie had underestimated the number of people who would be attending was an understatement. The line to get into the auditorium-like room zigzagged around the halls of the resort. She tried not to let the shock show on her face but she was nervous for Brian. Hell, she was kind of nervous for herself.

They were escorted in through a side entrance. "Señor Brian, follow me," a man said. Pablo walked by at that moment and gave Lizzie a thumbs-up and then handed Brian a drink. Brian didn't hesitate in downing it in one gulp, even though neither of them knew where Pablo had materialized from.

First, as was explained to her, was the book signing/ meet-and-greet. This meant that the line of fans waiting outside would come in, and one by one, he would sign their books and take photos. There was staff set up to help speed up the process, making sure the fans had their books open and were ready to go.

"And this is all for him only?" Lizzie whispered to Pablo in Spanish.

"Sí, señorita. He is B. Anderson," Pablo said as if the question were absurd. There were hearts in his eyes as he watched Brian take a seat and grab a couple of pens. "You can sit here, next to him. We set this up for you. I believe people will want your signature too. You are Gwinnie."

"I am not Gwinnie. I am not anyone. I'm moral support," she said. "Do you think I can get a drink too?"

"Claro que sí," Pablo said and went to fetch her a cocktail. Lizzie pulled up the chair next to Brian. Over the next two hours a sea of people walked up to him with books for signing and phones for selfies. During the first half hour, he was stilted and almost seemed pained. "You look like you hate them all," she whispered through the side of her mouth. "I wouldn't buy shit from you with that face."

He turned his head to her, eyes wide. "Not helping."

"Trying to give you some constructive criticism, snookums," she continued to whisper. "Smile."

He did and she jolted back a bit. "Oh Jesus. That looks demented." She reached for his face, even though people were watching their interaction, and squished his cheeks together with her hands, causing him to get funny fish lips. "Listen up, buttercup, you're B. Anderson, beloved author with the best teeth and smile in all of East Miami elementary, middle, and high schools. When I let go you better smile like you're enjoying these nice people who came all the way down here to see you and not like someone who has chronic explosive diarrhea."

"Kiss. Kiss. Kiss. Kiss," the crowd chanted and they both looked toward them, his face still squished up. She shrugged with both shoulders and gave him a loud kiss on his poofy lips before letting his cheeks go.

That seemed to loosen him up.

The second vodka soda helped too.

The rest of the signing went great. Lizzie politely declined to sign any books but agreed to the selfies. She didn't want to devalue Brian's signed copies by having an imposter's autograph next to his.

A melee of screaming fans jolted them both from what they were doing. From the side entrance Violet and her entourage had appeared. The starlet waved at her fans with the ease of someone who not only was used to being adored, but loved it.

"Scoot over, will ya, dear?" Violet said to Lizzie as she snapped her fingers together. A chair was slid in between Brian and Lizzie, and Violet sat down in all her grandeur. She did not do resort wear. She had on a tight short black dress and clear heels that looked uncomfortable and sweaty.

"You're in luck, ladies and gentlemen. Violet Gram will be joining the Q-and-A later," the moderator said from the stage.

"Yes. And I'll sign your books too," she said with a huge smile.

Brian looked over to Lizzie. This was his big day; she didn't want him obsessing over her feelings so she winked at him and mouthed, *It's fine.*

"Oh dear, I'm so sorry," Violet said to Lizzie. "You must be the fiancée."

Lizzie held out her hand. "Yes, I'm Lisette. It's nice to meet you."

Violet took her hand as if it were a limp noodle. "This must be so difficult for you, dear. Not everyone can handle stardom."

"I'm good," Lizzie said.

"So is my husband," Violet said quietly so only Lizzie could hear. "It comes with the territory."

"What does?" she asked.

"Don't be naive," Violet said and then focused back on the fans wanting her signature.

Perhaps some people did find Lizzie to be Brian's muse, but the actual Gwinnie had arrived and everyone all but forgot Lizzie was even in the room. Even though Lizzie generally felt confident with herself, sitting next to someone like Violet Gram would do a number on any woman's self-esteem. She/The Star was absolutely gorgeous, charismatic, and more self-assured than anyone Lizzie had ever met.

Violet reached for Brian's glasses and straightened them on his face. He grabbed her wrist to stop her.

"I'm engaged," he said.

"I'm married," she retorted.

Brian let out a defeated breath and pulled back, plastering on a smile when the next group stood in front of them.

By nine in the evening, the main doors were closed, and most people had taken a seat. "This is getting boring. I'm going to freshen up. I'll meet you on the stage, darling. Remember, I'm Gwinnie, the star of your little movie, so you need to play along. This is Hollywood and people want the chemistry on the screen to bleed into real life. Plus, I think we'd have a great time." She pushed her chair back. Her entourage came running over as she walked out the same door she'd entered an hour earlier.

Lizzie's head was spinning. Even knowing that Brian was not into Violet didn't make it any easier to be around. Partly because it was unfathomable to her that he didn't want Violet back. He tapped the chair Violet had been using and Lizzie moved over to sit beside him again. "I'm so sorry about that. I told you she was pushy."

"Understatement of the year."

The last person in line was the little girl she'd seen two days ago. "Oh, look, it's Rocio. The little girl I told you about." She had dark hair braided on either side, and she wore a little gingham dress and black shiny shoes that had seen better days.

"Hola Gwinnie," the little girl said.

"Mi amor, I told you, that's not really Gwinnie," the mom said in Spanish to her daughter. She then looked up to Lizzie and Brian. "She loves your books so much. We live in Mexico City and she found one of the books in a library. Some of the pages were missing but she started to help people in the neighborhood with different odd jobs and raised enough money to buy the book brand-new. We took five buses to get here, isn't that right, Rocio?"

"It was an adventure," Rocio said.

Brian stood and walked around the table and got down on his knee to speak to the girl. "I'm so glad you were able to make it all the way here," he said, then turned to Lizzie. "Translate that, please."

Lizzie did.

"What room are you staying in? I want to send you some more books and other fun stuff," he said, and Lizzie translated.

"No. We have friends who are picking us up tonight and taking us halfway back to our town."

"Well, maybe an address, then?" he said and then asked Pablo to write it all down. He signed Rocio's book, which she hugged tightly to her chest, and posed for an inordinate number of selfies, not caring that there was a roomful of people waiting for him.

"We need to get you on the stage, Señor Anderson."

"It was nice to meet you, Rocio."

"You too," she said with a smile that warmed Lizzie's heart. She was missing her two front teeth and her eyes crinkled with genuine delight.

"Pablo, please find them a room. The nicest one you have. I want to see if they'd stay the night or even a few days, if they can. All expenses paid. I mean food and everything. Then, I need to see how they can get back to their village in a less stressful way. Can you do that for me, please?"

"You are too kind, señor."

"Me? They are the ones that are kind. It is the least I can do."

This time Lizzie leaned forward and kissed him. There was no real need to put on a show. She'd done it because he melted her heart.

Brian

Brian had written the Invaders series because he'd enjoyed coming up with stories. Writing was a solitary hobby. And that's what it had been, a hobby, except that the more he got into the story the more he wanted to finish it. The new world he had created took over all his thoughts, during the writing of book one. It had been a labor of love. Pure joy. Had he not sold a single book, he wouldn't have cared, critiques and reviewers be damned. But it had been an overnight hit and he'd gotten a big book deal from it.

Then, books two and three had been written in a place of sadness because his grandparents had passed away. Instead of joy, writing had become an escape from the shitty reality of his life. After book three, the rest of the series had all been contractual obligations. Not that he hadn't enjoyed writing them, but that deep joy from book one had definitely been missing and the angst of two and three were also gone. He still loved to write, but he didn't love the pressure that came with it.

But now, miles and miles away from his small home office in Boston, seeing the joy in Rocio's face from something he had created made him want to cancel the rest of the evening, run back to his room, fire up his laptop, and create a world that would bring children like Rocio joy.

He was still thinking about the little girl when they escorted him up to the stage. He had not noticed that it was missing a podium. Instead, there was a table smack in the middle with a couple of chairs and microphones. The escort pulled out his chair and then shuffled Lizzie next to him. "Hmmm . . . this is weird. This is supposed to be a question-and-answer session. Louise drilled me on this a hundred times and told me what to expect, and this wasn't it."

"I thought this would be easier for you."

"This was your doing?"

"And Pablo's. I thought this would lessen the nerves. It makes it a little less formal, don't you think? Plus, I'm right here. We're just chatting with them. You're not the center of attention, you're just another person sitting down and chatting with a few friends."

He looked at her for a moment almost as if he were seeing

her for the first time. "You're amazing, Lizzie. Truly. Thank you." He took her hand in his and kissed the bottom of her wrist. Then Violet walked in and the moment dissipated because Violet would not be outdone by Lizzie. This time, however, Lizzie refused to be scooched over. Thank God for Pablo, who came running up and moved a chair to the other side of Brian, who was now sandwiched between Lizzie and Violet.

The moderator did stand at a podium off-center from the stage. He welcomed everyone to Cancún and specifically to Villas de Amor. He spoke about Brian and some of his accolades, then welcomed Violet.

"Without further ado, B. Anderson," he said, with a big swing of his arm.

Brian had put together a little speech, but maybe it was Lizzie or maybe it was Rocio's sweet smile—he crumpled it and pulled the mic from the center of the table closer to him. "Thank you all for coming. Gracias." He tried the Spanglish thing as best he could. "I hope you know that I write these books because of all of you. It's for you that I keep writing. I am overwhelmed and humbled by the turnout today and always. I thank you from the bottom of my heart. I appreciate all your questions and I know you're eagerly anticipating the next book. I think that this trip has rejuvenated me and hopefully you'll have book ten sooner rather than later, and you can thank this woman for it." He turned to Lizzie and gave her a kiss on the lips. The crowd oohed and ahhed. Lizzie was surely beet red. He turned back to the audience. "And if you don't mind, I have a special guest that I want to invite up here to sit with me. Rocio? Where are you, Rocio?"

"Aquí. Aquí!" The little girl hopped up on a chair all the way at the back.

"You want to join us?"

"Can I, Mommy?" she asked and the crowd laughed and then the little girl ran down the aisle up to the stage. Pablo, the absolute best ambassador ever, brought a chair and squeezed it between Violet and Brian. Violet wasn't happy. Pablo winked at Lizzie. The man was getting the best tip ever.

Rocio sat down right next to her idol.

Violet took the mic from Brian and slid it over to her. "It is so wonderful being here today with this amazing writer. He gave me Gwinnie, a part I've only ever dreamed of playing. Thank you for writing this part for me, darling. It's been the role of a lifetime."

Brian's brows furrowed but the moderators were already in the aisles, holding microphones to the fans, who held up their hands with questions.

"So the rumors about your muse were wrong? It was Violet?" That was the first question.

Brian was going to answer but Violet held the mic tightly. "Of course he wrote it for me. He just began this courtship with Ms. Alonso. He and I have been working together on this role for years. Isn't that right, darling?"

Brian smiled and nodded. Unfortunately (and fortunately,

because Brian hated public speaking) Violet took over most of the Q-and-A session. Wherever possible, she made it about herself. A few times, he had to correct her but for the most part she spoke and he let her. Under the table, he held Lizzie's hand, which she squeezed with annoyance.

When they asked intricate questions about his make-believe universe, Violet had no choice but to let Brian answer. There were also a lot of questions about Zeth and Gwinnie. Lizzie noticed he evaded those questions or would say "stay tuned"—even though Violet alluded to a love affair between the characters a few times, which Brian quickly quashed. Lizzie made a mental note to ask him more about that later.

Then the questions turned to the personal: "When's the wedding?" and "Will you move to London?"

"We haven't set a date," he said. "We're still figuring out the living arrangement," he said.

"We're shooting the movies stateside, so that would be impossible," Violet said at some point.

"Why aren't you wearing your ring?" someone asked.

"Oh, uh . . . I'm retaining liquid from all the margaritas, you know how that goes," Lizzie said with a coy smile, which everyone bought.

Around eleven the moderators started wrapping it up even though Lizzie was impressed at how well Brian was doing. She was exhausted. Pablo was chatting with Rocio's mother and by the smile on her face, Lizzie knew that he'd been able to set the two up in a room.

"See you tomorrow," Violet said and air-kissed them all. The woman seemed pissed off but Lizzie couldn't bring herself to give a shit.

"I kinda hate that you'll see her tomorrow or ever again."

"Ohhhh, you're jealous. Cute," Brian playfully replied.

She rolled her eyes at him. "You did great tonight," she said.

"Thanks to you."

"You did pretty good too. You know . . . with the writing the book and answering the questions 'n shit," she said with a laugh.

"You look tired. I'm just going to make sure they got Rocio and her mom settled in and that everything is set for the book auction on Sunday. I'll meet you in the villa?"

"If you're sure."

"I'm good. See you in a bit." He pulled her in and gave her a kiss on the lips that felt a bit too familiar, as if they'd done it a thousand times before. She secretly wished they could do it a thousand times again.

LIZZIE WOKE UP when she felt the bed dip and a body plop down. "Brian?" she croaked.

"Ugh."

She sat up and reached for the bedside lamp and turned it on. The six-foot man was half on the bed, half off. "What time is it?" Her phone said 1:47. "Did you just get back?"

He grumbled something incoherent. She tried to shake him awake but he just snored into the mattress. She slid out of the bed and, using all her force, flipped him over on his back.

"Eww . . . you smell like pure alcohol."

More grumbling.

With a shake of her head, Lizzie removed his shoes and socks, then undid his belt and unbuckled his pants. "Hips up." She heaved but the man was dead to the world. After a lot of effort, however, eventually she divested him of most of his clothes and got him to slide up the bed, where she co-cooned him in the sheets, like a burrito. Because of his angle, and the covers situation, she moved to his bed for the night.

Brian

Brian woke up to bile moving up his stomach, to his esophagus, and into his mouth. He ran to the bathroom and threw up the contents of everything he drank the night before, meaning, he vomited a lot because he drank the entire bar. Once his stomach was empty he rinsed his mouth out and expelled all the alcohol from his body via cold-ass shower. By the time he was wrapped in a hotel robe and walking to the kitchen he felt like a new man.

After drinking two full glasses of water, he ordered room

service while he brewed some coffee. He had slept in Lizzie's room, vaguely remembered her taking off his clothes and helping him settle in bed, but she hadn't slept with him. The door to his room was ajar. He leaned against the doorframe watching her, still in bed, with her laptop open on her legs, typing something. "Thank you," he said and she jumped, almost dropping the computer. She plucked out earbuds and held a palm over her chest.

"You scared the crap outa me. Jesus, how long have you been standing there?"

Brian pushed himself off the doorframe and walked toward her. "Just a moment. I was thanking you for getting me to bed. I think I drank too much."

"You think?" she said, closing her computer. "What happened after I left?"

"A group of readers were at the lobby bar and on my way here they asked me to join them for a drink and they just kept ordering drinks and more and more people joined the group. Then Violet showed up and I needed a stiff drink."

"Fame, free booze, and a hot movie star. It's a hard life you lead, Brian Anderson. How do you feel this morning?" she asked, scrunching up her cute button nose sympathetically.

"I'm fine. I don't get hungover."

"It's really, really hard to sympathize with your plight, you know?"

He laughed, loudly. She was also really funny. Beautiful, funny, and smart. He was going to miss her.

"So whatcha doing?" he asked, from the edge of the bed.

"I was getting some work done. Catching up on emails. I have hair and makeup in an hour in the bridal suite."

"What time is your flight tomorrow?" he asked.

"I have to be at the airport at nine A.M. You?"

"My flight's in the afternoon."

There was a thick air of silence in the room. Awkwardness had never been their thing. Anger, banter, passionate sex . . . that was their thing.

"Before you leave to do your lady stuff and then get caught up in wedding shit, I want to tell you that I don't think I could have handled the past couple of days without you, truly. Thank you."

"You were pretty great too."

He stood up and pulled her up with him, wrapping his arms tightly around her waist. "I think I'm going to miss you, Alonso."

"Ditto, Anderson."

He cupped her face in his hand and kissed her. It was tender and sweet and different from all their previous kisses. He felt his heart do a little thud.

A knock sounded, followed by a "Yoo-hoo, can I come in?"

"Come in, Pablo."

Pablo entered the villa and Lizzie was about to walk out but Brian stopped her. "I'm not done kissing you yet."

"But Pablo . . ."

"I don't want to kiss Pablo," he said and she chuckled. "The door is closed and he's in the kitchen. He'll be out of here in a minute."

Brian continued to kiss her until the front door opened and closed. She was practically writhing against him, clearly forgetting that a second ago she'd been worried about Pablo in the other room.

"Okay, let's go eat," he said.

"Wait, what!" she said, breathlessly, when he abruptly stopped. He took her by the hand to the kitchen. Pablo had done an excellent job. His ambassador/manservant/butler was going to get the biggest tip of his life.

"Oh my God," Lizzie whispered in disbelief, covering her mouth with her hand.

"Happy Valentine's Day," he said as she looked around the room. There were eleven vases with a dozen red roses in each. One dozen for each year between second grade and twelfth grade, when she alleged he'd ruined Valentine's Day for her.

"Brian . . ."

She looked up at him and seeing her eyes wet with unshed tears undid him.

"Don't you dare cry."

"I'm not crying," she said, with trembling lips and a big fat tear rolling down her round cheek.

"Of course not," he said, and wiped the tear with his

thumb. "This won't make up for the ruined Valentine's Days but maybe it can start a new trend. From Valentine's hate to looking forward to Valentine's Day?"

She nodded and then turned to him, wrapped her arms around his neck and spent the rest of the morning making love to him. He secretly wished this wasn't the first and only February 14 they could enjoy together.

Lizzie

You're late," Mari said when Lizzie finally walked into the bridal suite.

"Your bridezilla is showing," Lizzie said.

"Ugh . . . you're right. I'm sorry."

Lizzie took Mari's hands in hers. "Everything is going to be perfect. You're marrying your perfect guy. Everything else doesn't matter."

"I know. I know." Mari hugged Lizzie tightly. "Tía Lily may or may not be drunk, so she's even mouthier than usual. Demi is upset that I'm not letting her live Insta our hair and makeup session. Maybe I want to let my bridezilla-flag fly but I can't if I'm being taped in front of thousands of strangers. And my mom and Gus's mom both decided on wearing red."

"Red's not bad."

"My wedding colors are red, cabernet red, because it's Valentine's Day and it's romantic but they're both wearing bloodred. It doesn't match plus they're going to look like bridesmaids. It's tacky."

Lizzie chuckled. "Well, you only have the one bridesmaid so . . ."

"You're in red, Demi's in red, I'm in white with red roses, that's elegant. Fifty percent of my guests in bloodred . . . not cute, Lizzie."

"Breathe, Mari. It's fine. It's all going to be fine."

"Lisette, you look . . ." Tía Lily walked into the room with her cane pointing at Lizzie rather than being used as support. "You had sex."

"Tía!" Mari gasped at the same time that Lizzie yelled, "Lily!"

Then Mari looked at her friend. "Wait, she's right. Did you have sex? That's why you're late, isn't it?"

"I plead the fifth."

"What is the fifth?" Tía Lily asked, swinging her cane between them.

"That means that I'm not answering, Tía Lily." Lizzie grabbed the cane and pushed it down. "I think you should sit and let me hold that glass for you."

"Get your own champagne," she said and Lizzie had to hold in a laugh. "In my time people didn't talk about sex so openly."

"You're the one talking about it openly, Tía!" Mari said, snickering.

"Was it that smart man you came to dinner with yesterday?"

"Of course. I don't just have sex with random men, Lily. His name is Brian."

"Well, it could have also been with the handsome one. The one with the sister. He likes you, you know."

"I knew it!" Demi picked that moment to walk back into the adjoining room.

"No. No. I didn't do anything with Jason." Lizzie put her palms up in surrender.

"But he would have if you let him," Tía Lily said, waggling her brows up and down.

"Tía, por favor!" Mari said. "You're not helping!"

"I did not sleep with Jason or flirt with Jason. He's with you. He likes you, Demi. It's so obvious how much he likes you," Lizzie said quickly. She hadn't noticed that, actually, but it wasn't the moment for truths. It was the moment to calm everyone down so that her best friend could have the drama-free perfect wedding she dreamed of. "Tell her, Mari. Maria, come here," Lizzie yelled into the adjoining room. "Doesn't Jason like Demi so much?"

"Yes. We all saw," Mari said just as Maria walked in with fat curlers all over her head.

"Qué? What did you say?"

"Didn't we all comment on how much Jason is into Demi?"

Maria's brows furrowed and Mari's and Lizzie's eyes widened. "Oh yes. Yes. He really likes you. So sweet how he, uh . . . holds your hand and takes your photos so you don't have to do selfies."

Tía Lily snorted.

Demi, bless her heart, said, "I thought he was looking at you too much during dinner and we had a big argument. It was our first fight, actually. But then he extended our stay for another three days and upgraded us to a villa. He wouldn't do that if he wasn't into me, right?"

"Right!" Lizzie said overzealously.

"No more alcohol for you, Tía," Mari said and snatched the flute from her hand.

"You can Instagram Live my makeup, if you'd like," Lizzie said to Demi.

"Really? Yay."

"You owe me," Lizzie whispered to Mari, who mouthed *thank you* to her best friend.

LIZZIE SAT IN the hotel room, a tripod with a ring light propped up right in front of her face. She had to smile throughout the hour-and-a-half-long process and pretend that she loved that Demi was an inch from her face, dabbing a sponge painfully and repeatedly over and over her skin, while explaining the process, meticulously, to her followers. "All these blemishes can easily be covered using this," she would say and put her palm out to the camera to show the product to her audience. "I'm not into heavy makeup, maybe a natural look," Lizzie tried to say but

Demi smiled in a way that Lizzie immediately understood meant she would do whatever she wanted and Lizzie had no say in the matter.

"Let's cover these dark circles, shall we?" Demi said into the camera.

The rest of the women were having their makeup done professionally by someone who was in the adjoining room and most likely not insulting them in the process. Lizzie wished she hadn't volunteered for this as Demi spoke about wings and cut creases.

Lizzie's phone rang repeatedly but Demi wouldn't let her answer: "We're live, sweetie. They'll have to wait."

Finally when she was done, Demi turned the chair to a mirror. "Ta-da!" Demi regaled her viewers.

"Oh . . ." Never had Lizzie worn this much makeup but it looked good. Very good. She looked like a glamorous version of herself, a nice change from her normal minimalist look.

"Girl, you know how many people would give their right arm for your dimples?"

"Really?" Lizzie asked, turning her face from side to side.

"Yes!" It was the only real compliment she'd received from the woman.

"I didn't even know I had cheekbones," she said, still amazed at what Demi had done. Demi said goodbye to her audience and disconnected her phone.

Almost immediately Lizzie's phone rang again while

Demi put away all her products. It was William. "Who are you and what have you done with my boss and best friend?" he said.

"What do you mean?"

"I saw you on IG Live. I almost fell off my bed. I didn't even know you knew what IG was."

"I do know what IG is and you know that because you follow me."

"Yes, and you post a photo of some weird-ass food every few months or repost some cute puppy photo, even though you don't own a dog. So, you can imagine my surprise to see you on IG Live. Live!"

"How did you even know?"

"I follow Demi and I got a notification she was going live. And you got glammed! How many times have I tried to get you to wear something other than nude lipstick or brown eyeshadow? But nooooo, you wouldn't do it. You go one weekend to Cancún and you're all decked out on V-Day of all days! Who are you?"

"It's a long story and it involves a stressed-out bride."

"I cleared your schedule this week because it's going to take you three days to catch me up on all things Brian, wedding, and Cancún."

"Deal. I miss you, Will. Next time, you have to come with me."

"Can't, baby girl. Someone has to stay and hold down the fort."

"Have you put any thought on what's next?" They'd discussed this many times but neither had made a decision. "Are you going to take the Italian job?"

"Don't know. I'm procrastinating."

"What if . . . what if . . . you came to work for me?"

"What?"

"I don't know. I've been thinking about it and maybe I want to consult on my own. Decide what jobs to take and where to take them. It could all blow up in my face or—"

"Or it could be super successful. You're the best in the biz, Lisette."

"We'll talk about it some more when I get back. I want you to think it through carefully. I'd hate for you to go down with the ship if I fail."

"You don't fail. That wouldn't even be a concern," he said.

"Thanks for that, Will." They didn't normally get deep or vulnerable with each other and she wasn't sure what else to say. *Now look who was being socially awkward.* "I really don't know how I could've gone through this week without the great job you've been doing over there. So thank you for that."

"Cancún agrees with you, Lizzie."

I think it's Brian. Brian agrees with me.

But she didn't say that out loud.

Chapter Ten

Brian

While Lizzie had gone to get her hair and makeup done, Brian had gone for a jog. Any residual alcohol in his system was sweated out of his body. He could feel rather than see Violet approach from his peripheral. Fuck. How did the woman know he was out for a jog? He did not want her around. Passive-aggressively, he pretended to be in the runner's zone and cranked up his earbuds louder and continued to pound the sand. Unfortunately, the pretense could only go so far, especially since paparazzi were nearby snapping photos.

The faster he ran, the faster she went. Damn it, she was in good shape. Eventually, he had to slow down to a walk, his hands on his waist as his pulse and breathing regulated. "You can sure run," he admitted to her.

"It's how I keep my figure."

"So, the husband doesn't run?" he asked.

"Scott has his own hobbies. Running isn't one of them. How about the girl, the fiancée? Where is she?"

Did Lizzie run? No, he didn't think so. Hell, did she do any sort of physical activity other than ride his cock with stellar enthusiasm?

"Nah," he said.

She grabbed his wrist and stopped him. "We have a lot in common, Brian. You have to admit we'd have a good time."

He exhaled, fully aware there was a small group of on-lookers watching them. "I don't mess with married women, Violet."

"It's not a real marriage," she retorted.

"I like you, Violet, but not in that way."

"Do you know how many men in Hollywood would give it all up to be seen with me?"

"I'm sure. You're gorgeous, smart, talented, but I'm just a quiet introvert from Boston. This is all bigger than anything I ever wanted."

"Our relationship would be mutually beneficial. People want to see us together. Zeth and Gwinnie in real life."

"I'm not Zeth and you're not Gwinnie. Those are characters that I wrote."

"Edward and Bella, Robert and Kristen, were one and the same. Brad and Angelina in *Mr. and Mrs. Smith*. I can name so many actors that fell in love and their movies skyrocketed to number one at the box office. Plus, it would be a helluva good time," she said, taking a step toward him.

"I'm not doing this with you, Violet. I don't want us to be on bad terms but I also don't want to lead you on in any way."

"One photo of the two of you!" a man with a camera that had a long lens yelled from the boardwalk.

"Kiss. Kiss," another one yelled.

Violet, who was always in character, turned to the press. "Our author is shy," she said, her finger running down his chest. He took a step back.

"I said no, Violet." This time he knew he would piss her off because there was no room for interpretation. He did not want her.

Unfortunately, that just angered the woman and before he knew it, she grabbed the back of his neck and pulled him in for a kiss. He pushed her off him before stomping away, but it was too late, the photo had been taken.

"I know you're not really engaged to that woman," Violet yelled, which made him miss a step and almost tumble onto the sand.

He turned and marched back. "Why would you say that?"

"From your reaction just now. You didn't deny it. I knew it was too weird that you just happened to come here with a fiancée."

"Buy it or don't. It's not my problem."

"It will be when I drop out of the next movies and stop doing any PR for this one."

"This is beyond crazy, Violet. Do whatever you want to do. I'm done." He turned and walked away before he said something truly hurtful to this vicious woman who probably had never been rejected in her life.

His phone buzzed in his pocket.

> **Lizzie:** Can you meet me at the wedding? I don't think I'll be able to make it back to the villa on time. We're running a little late. Long story involving Instagram and a tipsy octogenarian.

He smiled, even if a minute ago he'd been seething. He'd laughed more in the last few days than he probably had all year.

> **Brian:** Sure. No problem.

He looked her up on Instagram, wanting to see what she was blabbering about.

> **Brian:** You need to update your IG. Your last post was about the series finale of Game of Thrones.

> **Lizzie:** Stalker

> **Brian:** I wanted to read the long version of the IG incident.

> **Lizzie:** It's humiliating. I'll share the link after my third drink later this evening.

He needed to tell her about the kiss the moment he saw her. If she found out online, she'd cut off his balls.

THE CEREMONY WAS a small affair by the beach. He waved at the groom's and bride's parents, who he'd already met, watched Jason sit on the groom's side, next to a woman who he had yet to meet. Brian sat on the third and last row on the bride's side, which meant there was no one in front of him.

"Scooch closer!" Tía Lily said to him from the first row. She yelled it, her voice echoing through the sound of the wind and crashing waves. "Why are you all the way back there? Maybe you're not that smart after all."

"Tía!" Mari's mother said and gave Brian an apologetic look.

"They have more people than we do. If that nincompoop is sitting all the way back there, it looks like we have even less." She was flailing her cane around again. "If we all get close together, it'll seem like we have more."

"This isn't a competition. It's only Gus's parents, the best man's wife, and Jason over there," Ramon said.

"Yes, that's four. We're three!" Lily said.

Brian did not want to get on Tía Lily's bad side; as it was

he was already labeled a nincompoop, so he moved one row up. She winked at him in return.

The music began. Brian turned.

Demi came out first. She smiled at her family and stopped and posed for Jason, who took a photo, likely for her social media. Then, he saw Lizzie.

His breath was expelled from his lungs.

He'd never been sucker punched, but he had to assume this was how it would feel.

Lisette Alonso was walking down the aisle. The wind had unraveled whatever hairdo she'd had done, which was fine because she looked absolutely breathtaking with her hair blowing behind her. She wore a long strapless dress the color of red wine. The material was thin and flowy. She had on more makeup than he'd ever seen her wear before but still, it wasn't unnatural-looking. She looked like a glammed-up version of Lizzie. Her lips matched her dress and she had a big expressive smile on her face.

She walked alongside a man he hadn't met before but assumed was the best man, who had arrived that morning. The man said something to her that caused her to throw her head back and laugh that hearty laugh of hers, exposing those deep dimples.

Never had he seen a more beautiful woman in his life. As soon as their eyes met she winked at him and he knew instantly that the way she looked at him at that moment would be etched forever into his brain. One day he'd be as old as Tía Lily and the memory of Lizzie, with her big open smile and deep dimples, would be as fresh as it was today.

Yeah yeah yeah . . . the wedding march sounded and the bride walked down. People shed tears but Brian missed it all because he wasn't looking at Mari, his eyes remained on Lizzie throughout the entire ceremony.

Lizzie looked back at him too, which wasn't lost on him. As she stood next to her best friend, her gaze on him said a thousand words. He could practically hear her saying, "Looking good, Anderson." Or something snarky like "I have sand in places one should not have sand. Remind me that beach weddings aren't as great as you'd imagine." That last one would be for his ears only. And he would then give her a list of reasons why beach weddings were the shit, just to rile her up.

". . . you may now kiss the bride."

Lizzie was wiping tears from her face. She wasn't a cute crier, mostly because she tried so hard to keep the tears inside that her nose flared and her plump bottom lip did an unattractively adorable pout thing.

The bride and groom walked out as the photographer snapped photos. Then Lizzie and the best man walked down the aisle, and finally Demi. The photographer escorted the small group straight back to the wedding arch for formal photos.

He waited for her, watching her laugh with her friend and pose with the wedding party. It was a truly beautiful wedding.

"Oh my God, this humidity and all this makeup . . .

ugh . . . my face is literally melting off. Ewww . . ." she said as she walked to him, absently kissed his lips, and then handed him the small bouquet of roses. A waiter came by with some champagne and Lizzie plucked out a napkin from the tray instead of a drink. "I need to blot," she said, and then patted her face gently. "Look. This is gross." She turned the napkin and there was makeup on it. "It's all that foundation. I must look crazy."

"Well, if you'd let me get a word in, I was going to say how beautiful you looked."

"Oh, well then." She wrapped her arms around his neck, which surprised him, since they were in front of everyone and she wasn't exactly the poster child for public displays of affection. "I'm all ears."

He chuckled, but then all humor left him. "Seriously. When I saw you walk out you took my breath away."

"Thank you," she said and kissed him, followed by a wipe of his lips. "Lipstick, sorry."

He shrugged and went in for another kiss.

"If everyone's ready, I'll escort you to the reception," the wedding planner said to the party. They broke the kiss (reluctantly) and followed everyone to the reception.

In the back of his mind there was something he wanted to tell her, but he couldn't remember, for the life of him, what it was.

"RECEPTION" WASN'T THE correct word for a party of thirteen. But they did go to a room set up with a long table full of red roses and a small dance floor. The décor was Valentine's Day themed, of course. There were candy hearts as favors as well as Valentine's Day cards, like the ones kids exchanged in grade school. There were also a lot of rose petals and candles everywhere.

As always, Lizzie was the center of attention. Aside from the bride of course. Well, Tía Lily did give Lizzie a fight for her money. When it was time for the maid of honor speech, something Brian hadn't seen her talk about or even practice, she just started to talk. He wondered if she'd written it out or if it was off the cuff. She was funny and heartfelt and hit all the right notes. All the women were in tears, including Lizzie. Hell, Brian had a lump in his throat.

Gus's best man began with "Damn. I should've gone first. Following her sucks."

Brian agreed and everyone chuckled.

"Come 'ere, baby, that was so good," Brian said, pulling her chair out and dabbing her eyes with a napkin.

She kissed him softly and then they turned their attention back to the best man.

They sat and enjoyed dinner while a small three-piece band played in the background. There was a lot of laughter, great food, and love.

Thankfully, Jason and Demi were sitting at the other end of the table and Brian didn't have to watch the man stare at Lizzie all night, even if he felt his eyes on her.

After dinner, the newlywed couple stood and had their first dance. There were more tears from the women.

"Remember the first day we met?" Brian asked Lizzie. There may have been other people at the table but they sat with their chairs turned toward each other, knee to knee, drinks in hand, talking.

"How can I forget. Valentine's Day, nothing like this one though. You ripped the card I so graciously gave you."

"I know. It was a bad day. My mom loved to do those PTA-mother things like cards and bake brownies. Grandma didn't do any of that and it was my first day. I was generally sad about having to move to a new city, I was an orphan, and then you came along with nothing but sunshine and happiness and it just pissed me off."

She reached for his face. "Brian . . ." Her voice cracked. "I'm sorry. I didn't think about—"

"No. Don't apologize. You were a kid. Shit time for me to bring this up—"

"You suck at reading the room, Anderson."

He laughed. "I'm only saying it because I want you to know that you pissed me off because you were so fucking awesome and kind and cute with that big red bow on your head. And even if we never see each other after this week, at least you'll know that I did not hate you. Ever. Jealous, envy . . . maybe. Hate, absolutely not."

"You remember my red bow?"

"That's what you got from my little heartfelt speech?"

"It was in second grade. That was like twenty-six years ago. My abuela made that for me. I loved that headband."

"I know. You wore it all the time."

"I didn't hate you either. I don't actually hate anyone."

"You didn't like me, though."

"Well, you never explained these things to me. I didn't know you were going through a tough time, although I feel like the world's biggest asshole for not realizing it. You didn't tell me that you were protecting me from other kids."

"And you thought I'd stood you up for prom. You had a lot of reasons to dislike me. But I hope that's not the case anymore."

"You know it's not the case anymore, 'snookums,'" she said, and slapped him playfully on the shoulder, but he grabbed her arm and pulled her closer to him.

"I wish you lived closer. I wish I could do relationships. I think with you, I could try," he admitted. Had he drunk too much? This was a big admission and he wasn't sure how she would take it.

"Brian . . ." she whispered, her eyes wide.

"Dance with me," he said. She looked around, having been so enthralled by their conversation she'd missed that the couples were dancing. Everyone except Tía Lily.

"Yes," she said and he stood, took her hand, and led her to the dance floor, where the small band played an instrumental version of "Groovy Kind of Love" by the Mindbenders.

He twirled her around a few times, then brought her close, swaying to the song. The rest of the evening was perfection. The couple didn't do a lot of the traditional wedding things, there wasn't a garter toss, although at one point, as Lizzie walked to the bar, Mari said, "Hey Lizzie, heads up!" When Lizzie looked, Mari had tossed her the bouquet, which Lizzie caught.

Lizzie

*B*rian was in the restroom and Demi was doing the Macarena with the other women, including Tía Lily. Lizzie's feet throbbed from the heels she'd worn and she had to sit for a while. A vodka soda was placed in front of her just as Jason took Brian's seat.

"I know you're avoiding me."

"Actually, I'd forgotten you were here." It was the absolute truth. She'd been so consumed by Brian all thoughts of Jason had faded away.

"So you two, you're really serious, huh?" he asked.

"Not really your business." Mostly, she said it because she didn't want to lie to him. Hell, she didn't want to lie at all.

"Fair enough." Lizzie brought the drink to her lips. "Do you ever come to the States? Maybe we can catch up, really catch up, next time you're in town."

"Seriously, Jason. You're here with Demi and you're making plans with me?"

"Demi and I are just having fun. It's not serious."

"Does she know that? You're kind of an expert at mixed signals. You say 'love' but you really mean you love getting your rocks off with other women."

"Everything okay?" Brian asked, walking back and taking a sip of Lizzie's drink.

"Sure is, buttercup. Jason was just going to dance 'YMCA' with Tía Lily." She said it loud enough that Lily heard and smiled at Jason.

"You are one lucky albeit fucked guy, Brian. She's an amazing woman but once she's done, she's done for good." Jason said it sincerely. "I'm sorry, Lizzie. For everything. I just wanted you to know that. I understand why you left, you deserved better and I screwed things up. I would have liked to tell you privately but you refuse to give me any time so that's what I wanted to say—I'm sorry. I was an immature idiot and I royally fucked up."

It was the first sincere thing he'd said to her all weekend.

"I appreciate that, Jason." It was something she needed to hear. And had she stayed at least ten minutes after she caught him in bed with someone else, she may have heard the apology five years ago, but she didn't do that. She cut and ran, which had always been the easiest thing for her to do. She did it after her mother died by moving to London and after the breakup with Jason.

Maybe, just maybe, running away from the problem and grief didn't solve anything but only tightened the walls around her heart.

At the end of the evening, Lizzie hugged everyone and

said heartfelt goodbyes. She had to head to the airport early and wouldn't see anyone in the morning. "Have a great honeymoon."

"And have a safe flight! Thank you for coming all the way to Mexico on your worst day of the year while you're in the middle of a huge project at work."

"Anything for you, Mari," she said to her best friend.

"I think you should keep him," Mari said, looking over Lizzie's shoulder. She turned her head to watch Brian and Tía Lily laugh about something. "I've never seen you this way. You're totally into him and he can't keep his eyes off you. Don't let love pass you by, Lizzie."

"Love? This is a weekend fling."

"It's not," Mari said and gave her friend a final kiss and hug.

Who was she kidding? She was dreading having to say goodbye. She'd warned him multiple times not to fall in love with her and she'd gone and fucked things up by falling in love with him.

Lizzie had a smile on her face while they walked back to their villa, even though her feet throbbed from the heels.

"I need to ask the front desk a quick question," he said as they crossed the lobby.

"I'll wait right here, if you don't mind. My feet are killing me."

He kissed her briefly and went to the lobby as she sat down on a couch to take off her shoes.

"So fake girlfriend, huh?" A woman wearing big sunglasses and a fabulous-looking hat sat down next to her. It was Violet. She recognized the star even with the glasses. Her security detail was discreetly close by. It was late in the evening and the lobby was mostly empty.

"Hi," Lizzie said, unsure as to where the conversation was headed. "I'm not fake—"

"Let's cut the bullshit. He told me when we were together this morning. I know you're just pretending. He's going places and you're in the way of that. If these movies take off the way I know they will he's going to be the next big thing and he doesn't need some corporate nobody by his side. No offense, honey, but you may not care that you're in my way, but you're also in his and he's too nice of a guy to tell you."

"Listen, Violet. I don't care who you are or how famous you may be. I'm not going to sit here and let you offend me. If he wanted you he wouldn't have needed to pretend to be with me just to get you off his back," she said and began to slip her shoes back on her feet. She was shaking with anger.

"You may be pretend but I'm the real thing, sweetie." Violet stood up before Lizzie was able to finish putting on her shoes. Brian was walking their way. "Enjoy him one last time. I don't mind sharing. Hell, we've already shared him this weekend." She waved to Brian. "See you on the rest of the tour, honey."

"What did she want?" Brian asked Lizzie as Violet walked away.

It had been such a great evening. Did she want to ruin it with the bullshit Violet was spewing? It was obviously the way of a desperate woman. Lizzie had no reason to believe anything Violet had said.

"Just some shitty acting. Come on. Let's go to bed." She took Brian's hand and they went to their villa.

BRIAN HAD ASKED about Rocio to make sure she and her mother were comfortable and that all their expenses were paid. He also inquired about possibly taking a flight to London tomorrow. Would he be that bold? Could he?

The air was heavy around them, both avoiding having to say goodbye. Or was it something that Violet had said to her? Lizzie wasn't someone to stay silent. Had Violet upset her, she'd surely have said so, wouldn't she?

They had agreed that it didn't need to end tomorrow but they were both realists and the reality was that they lived in different countries. It wouldn't be the same after today; they'd drift apart and that would be that.

"I'm glad it was a beach wedding," he said, finally breaking the silence. "Otherwise, I would have been severely underdressed."

"You don't normally pack a tuxedo when traveling?"

They both laughed and then more silence. He opened their villa's door and was about to say something, but she pulled him inside and kissed him senselessly. She didn't want to talk. There was nothing more to say. If this went past tonight, it would be wonderful and she was open to it, but she didn't want to talk logistics and specifics. Not today, anyway. They could FaceTime about it once she arrived in London.

"If I didn't know any better you were trying to shut me up, for once," he said as he licked down her neck.

"I want to make sure that I remember what great sex feels like."

He lifted her up, cupping her ass cheeks and gently placing her on his bed. "We're going to talk even if it's while I'm balls-deep inside of you," he said, pushing her dress up, exposing a lacy thong, which he proceeded to slide down her legs.

"No. You're going to ruin this with words."

"I'm going to visit you in London," he said, kissing the inside of her thighs. "You're going to visit me in Boston. We'll have phone sex in between." He reached her center just as he said this and her body arched upward.

"I can't do casual, Brian," she said while writhing. "If you cheat on me, I can't do that."

He stopped licking her wet center and slid up to her face. "Now, why would you say that?"

"You see, this is why this wasn't the best time to talk." She tried to push him with the heel of her foot. She needed more tongue or fingers . . . she needed something and he wasn't doing anything but looking at her. "Please, Brian . . ."

"Talk to me first."

"I'm not Violet. I can't compete with that or with any other rich and famous bombshell that's going to be thrown your way. I'm just Lisette and a few days ago, you didn't even like me."

That was it, her insecurities were out there for him to crush if he so desired. A tear actually slid down her cheek and she tried to turn her face away from him but he wouldn't let her. He kissed the tear away and then kissed her lips. "I don't want Violet or anyone else. I want you. Only you."

"You said you didn't want a relationship."

"That was before."

"Before what? You said it yesterday."

"I was stupid yesterday," he said, tulle and chiffon covering his face as he slid his way down her body again. He used his shoulders to hold her thighs open and with his fingers, he opened her lips and began to lick and suck her until she felt she was hovering over the bed in a life-altering orgasm.

Her eyes were still shut in bliss when he flipped her to her stomach and unzipped her dress and practically ripped it off her. He stood and took off all his clothes and was back on her before she had a chance to look at him. And boy, did she want to look at him. She wanted to remember each and every inch of his body.

He guided himself to her entrance and pushed. "Oh . . ." she said, her eyes opening as she took his face in her hands and kissed him over and over; it was a messy kiss because she was having a hard time concentrating on kissing while his hips were thrusting roughly into her.

He snaked his arm protectively around her waist. She'd never had such passionate sex before. His body was so tightly held against hers, she wasn't sure how he was thrusting. Each and every inch of their bodies were flush together. "I'm coming, baby," he cried as he pushed one last time into her.

"Happy Valentine's Day, Lizzie."

"Happy Valentine's Day, Brian."

Chapter Eleven

Lizzie

Lizzie couldn't sleep.

She tossed and turned all night. She felt a sense of foreboding. It was the long plane ride back home that had her worried. She didn't enjoy flying.

It wasn't that she would have to say goodbye to Brian in a few hours. He had told her he wanted to take her to the airport, even if it meant he'd have to wake up early and then drive back later for his own flight.

He hadn't just been the best thing that happened to her all weekend. He was the best thing that had happened to her in a long time. He reminded her of home and it had been years since home felt like a good memory. Every time she thought of home she thought of her mother, who she missed every single day. Or of Jason, who had broken her heart into a million little pieces.

When she realized sleep was not going to happen, she rolled over and grabbed her phone. Brian reached for her, even though he was sound asleep. He pulled her toward his chest and held her tightly. How had she been against cuddling? Cuddling with Brian was a close second to sex with Brian.

With his arms tightly around her, she checked her emails and awkwardly answered some of the messages with her one free hand.

She had a couple of Facebook, Twitter, and Instagram notifications. Most were from Demi's tags. She read some of the comments, embarrassed at having been recorded. She was also tagged in a bunch of photos of Brian. Her followers on most social media platforms had quadrupled. She scrolled through the notifications and most were coming from a specific photo on Instagram. She clicked on it and felt her heart crack. After understanding that most of their past arguments were misunderstandings, pranks, or immaturity, she should have given him the benefit of the doubt. That's what she should have done. However, it was hard to do that when men continuously let her down.

On her screen was a photo of Brian and Violet. It had been taken yesterday while she'd been doing her hair. In one photo they'd been jogging, the next one, they were kissing. *We've already shared him this weekend.* Her vile words resonated. The headline said: "B. Anderson caught in a compromising position."

She sat up carefully, not wanting to wake him yet. She read through the comments.

"*It's Violet Gram, they have chemistry.*"

"*Wowza, look at that kiss.*"

"*She's married. Anderson's a dog.*"

"*He was just using that poor other woman to get Violet jealous.*"

"*It's about time.*"

"*Poor thing. She was plain, bless her heart.*"

To make things worse, there was an article on TMZ: "Violet Gram confirms she's leaving her husband of eight years for B. Anderson, creator of the Invader series." Lizzie clicked on the article and read, "This is a hard time for my family and privacy is appreciated." When asked a more probing question, Violet answered, "Yes, the heart wants what it wants and Brian and I are over the moon."

Her eyes watered. She thought Jason had caused her pain all those years ago, but she hadn't known pain. This was agony.

Quietly, she slid out of bed. She brushed her teeth and got dressed. She had packed the night before, so there wasn't anything left to do. She looked at the vases of roses that still sat on the table. She had an urge to take each and every vase and throw them at the wall and watch them shatter, like her heart. But she didn't want to talk to Brian and throwing eleven glass vases against the wall would wake him and all the neighboring villas.

Instead, she grabbed a handful of roses, broke them in half, and tossed them in the trash. When there wasn't any more space in the trash can, she just broke them and left them all over the table. It wasn't until she left the villa and was in the cab to the airport that she noticed that her hands were bleeding from all the thorns.

It wasn't half as painful as the way her heart bled.

Chapter Twelve

Brian

*B*rian woke up feeling euphoric. He stretched his arms, still feeling the effects of the best sex of his life. Every time with Lizzie had been the best sex of his life. It would only get better every time.

He had done exactly what she had asked him not to do—he'd fallen in love with her. He was absolutely sure about it. He didn't want to part with her. In fact, he was going to find a flight to London and go with her, if she didn't find it too clingy. Although, at this point, he felt clingy. He wanted her. All of her. All the time.

He turned and reached for her, but her side of the bed was empty. And cold. His brows furrowed and he reached for his phone. It was ten-twelve in the morning. Her flight left at nine. He sat up abruptly. Shit.

"Lizzie?" he yelled, knowing she wasn't there. He'd told her he wanted to take her to the airport and she'd protested, saying it would be too much work for him. Shit, she'd left and he hadn't told her all the things he wanted to say. He plopped back down.

Damn, stubborn woman.

He called her but of course, it went straight to voicemail since she was probably somewhere over the Atlantic by now. "You left without saying goodbye. Have a safe flight and call me as soon as you land."

He ordered room service and then went to take a quick shower.

"Yoo-hoo . . ." It was Pablo, half an hour later as Brian was finishing dressing.

"Come in. I'll be right out."

"Oh my God, señor!" Pablo said, alarm in his voice.

Brian came out of his room, the shirt not fully on his body yet. "What in the hell?"

The two men stood for a moment looking at the mess. There were broken roses all over the table and blood smeared all over the white linen chairs.

"I will have this cleaned up in no time, señor," Pablo said, quickly making a call. Brian hadn't moved. "Señor? Are you okay?"

"I . . . I don't know." He picked up a rose from the floor but it broke in half, leaving him with a sad-looking dead rose in his hand. "Is there a way of finding out if she made it onto her flight?"

"I can call and see if she made it to the airport."

"Yes, please do that," Brian said and then took the trash can and started to press down on the flowers sticking out from it, but it was pointless.

Two room attendants walked in a moment later with a big black garbage bag and within minutes they'd cleared all the flowers. They were discreet, not asking any questions or making any comments. Next they scrubbed the white chairs clean. Finally, they removed the vases and wiped off all the water that had dripped onto the table and floor. It was as if nothing had happened, which felt a lot like the truth. Lizzie had packed up and left, as if nothing had happened. As if he'd dreamt it all.

Except everything had happened. He felt as if his insides had imploded.

Brian just stood there watching. What had happened? He was about to tell her he loved her, something he was certain she also felt, and then she'd done the exact thing he asked her not to do. She had run away.

"Señor, the concierge confirmed that Ms. Alonso was in a taxi and was dropped off at the airport."

"Thank you, Pablo."

"And señor, I think you should see this." The man flipped the phone over and a photo of Violet and Brian kissing was on the screen. It had millions of hits and thousands of comments, none of which he wanted to read. Fuck. He'd completely forgotten to tell Lizzie. It had been on his mind to tell her the moment he saw her but he'd been distracted by her beauty and by mind-blowing sex.

If she'd stayed and listened he would have been able to explain. "Fuck!" he roared. He wanted to call her and explain but she'd left. The first sign of a problem and she'd left. That was fucked up. It was the one thing he'd asked of her, not to run.

He grabbed his suitcase and started to throw his clothes inside. "Señor, let me help."

"No, Pablo, thank you. I'd like to be alone." He looked for his wallet, opened it, and handed Pablo a wad of cash. He had more money now than he knew what to do with and Pablo had been extraordinary. "Gracias for everything," he said to Pablo. He had already made sure to tell Louise to send Pablo's son swag from the books and from the movie next week.

"This is too much, señor."

"No, Pablo. It's not." He gave the man a tight handshake but Pablo went in for a hug. "If you're ever in Boston, Pablo . . ."

"Gracias, señor."

As soon as Pablo left, Brian finished throwing all his shit into the bags, desperate to get the hell out of the room that still smelled like the woman he'd fallen in love with and who had left him without so much as giving him the benefit of the doubt. He called the concierge to ensure there was a cab waiting outside; the last thing he wanted was to see anyone, particularly Violet. He actually hated her at that moment.

When he arrived home, there were news cameras all over his front yard. As a private person, this was the last thing he needed or wanted.

"Fuck," he roared, tossed money to the cabbie, and stepped out of the car.

"Brian. Brian. Would you like to make a statement?" one reporter asked.

A mic was shoved into his face. "How do you feel about being called a home-wrecker?"

"Do you think this scandal will affect sales?"

"Is this a PR stunt to boost sales?"

He unlocked his front door and slammed it shut, then proceeded to close all the blinds.

His phone rang as he took out a beer from the fridge. He needed to unpack but right now, he didn't want to do anything. His friend Greg was calling.

"Hello," he barked out.

"Yo, you're sleeping with Violet Gram? I thought you didn't want to go there. Dude, she is hot! *H-O-T*. But not the best career move."

"I didn't and I don't. It was all fake. I didn't kiss her."

"What I don't understand is why one week you're engaged all of a sudden and a few days later you're kissing Violet."

Brian took a long pull of his beer and sat down. "Lizzie, my *fake* fiancée"—he emphasized "fake"—"was just a friend trying to help me get Violet off my back." "Friend" hadn't been the correct word at the time but he didn't need to go into all the details.

"It must be hard being you," Greg said.

"Har-har. Violet set me up. She kissed me in front of reporters, I pushed her away, but I got screwed over anyway. It's online so it must be true."

"And the fake fiancée?" Greg asked.

"She saw it online. Got pissed off and left me without a word. I asked her not to believe the shit she saw online without talking to me about it first, and she didn't bother."

"There's photos of you and Violet Gram making out."

"And they're fake," he repeated.

"And you think that's something a woman is just going to let go because you told her not to believe it in advance?"

"Well . . . yeah." It sounded stupid and impossible now that he thought about it. He would have jumped to conclusions had it been the other way around.

"It wasn't fake for you anymore," Greg deadpanned.

Was he that transparent? "How'd you guess?"

"This is the most riled up I've ever heard you. You texted me more this last weekend than you did in the last year. You even posted on social media."

That statement reminded Brian of something similar his grandmother had once said to him.

"You should be more patient with that girl. She's a good girl."

"She's a pain, Grandma," he'd said angrily.

"If she was just a pain, you wouldn't get so mad. You'd ignore her like you do most everything else." Grandma had always said he ignored things but it wasn't that he ignored things, it was that he didn't like being the center of attention, he liked to stay in his comfort zone. But Lizzie challenged him. She was someone who you couldn't ignore. And the last thing they'd said to each other all those years back, or rather, the last thing she'd said to him, with tears in her eyes, was a memory still ingrained in his soul. Now he understood why.

IT WAS THE last day of high school and the entire class had gone to a party at Tropical Meadows, a park where some of the kids hung out. Someone had snuck beers and everyone was letting loose and saying their goodbyes before they all parted ways. He'd seen Lizzie there, which was the first shock, and then he'd seen her with a red plastic cup full of beer, which had been the second shock. She was a Goody Two-shoes and he'd never imagined her doing something like that. They'd ignored each other all night long and then when he'd noticed she was a little tipsy at the end of the night, he'd gone to offer her a ride home. Whether he liked her or not, he wasn't a total asshole, couldn't live with himself if she drove home drunk.

Except the moment he'd made the offer, her back straightened and her eyes narrowed and she'd said, "I don't want a ride from you. I don't want anything from you."

He'd held out both hands, taken aback by her anger. It was sharper than usual. He could see how much she hated him—actually hated him—for the first time ever.

"Fine. Be careful getting home," he said and as he turned to walk away she yelled, "Fuck you, Brian Anderson."

She missed Sunday dinner that weekend and he never saw her again, until now in Mexico.

He hadn't known about the senior prom prank the weekend before. Now, he wished he had. He wished he could go back and comfort the young woman who'd been hurt unnecessarily. The one who apparently liked him enough to agree to go out with him and had been stood up. If he put himself in her shoes, he'd hate him too. Of course the woman had trust issues; she'd been abandoned, left, disappointed by all the men in her life. Damn it. She didn't deserve that. She was sensitive, but didn't want the world to see it. He saw it though, and he loved that he was the only one who knew that about her.

And the way she riled him up—it made him feel alive. She challenged him, showed him that life was worth living with passion and gusto. And she believed in love even when she'd been hurt.

Lisette Alonso was amazing and he needed her in his life.

"I'M NOT SURE if the right phrase is 'riled up' or 'pissed off,'" he said, agreeing with Greg.

"Damn. You fucked up."

"Indeed," he said, polishing off the beer and grabbing a second one from the fridge.

"What are you going to do to fix this?"

"I don't know but it has to be huge," he said. He knew he needed to fix it because spending the rest of his life without Lizzie was not an option.

After they said their goodbyes and hung up, Brian sat back with the beer in his hand. The desk in the corner of the room had stacks of draft copies of his next book. He always printed them because it was easier to review a draft if he had a hard copy in his hand. They'd all sucked. They had marks all over them; some had pages ripped out and others lay crumpled in the wastebasket. He hadn't turned any in because he hated them all. Something was off and he didn't know if he had been trying to avoid the Zeth and Gwinnie big romantic gesture because they weren't ready to finally be together or because he didn't want to merely pander to the fans. He wanted it to happen organically and writing in a fishbowl was becoming increasingly difficult.

He put down the beer bottle and grabbed the last copy he'd printed and started reading it. Damn it, Gwinnie truly resembled Lizzie. Both were hardheaded and unreasonable. If Lizzie wouldn't have run away and instead listened . . .

"Urgh!" he grabbed a pen and started to write.

And with that in mind, the ending of his new book began to make sense.

Finally.

Lizzie

*D*amn it, William! Where's my one o'clock? My two o'clock is here and now suddenly I'm double-booked," Lizzie yelled into the receiver.

Without a response, William hung up and forty-nine seconds later he walked into Lizzie's office without even so much as a knock and locked the door behind him.

"Boss or friend?"

"Boss," Lizzie barked without looking up from her computer.

"Okay, boss it is." He cleared his throat. "Ms. Alonso, it is, unfortunately, out of my control that your one o'clock is running late or that your two o'clock is early. May I suggest you meet with the two o'clock now, since she's here, and then when, or if, the one o'clock shows up, he'll have to wait until you finish with your two o'clock."

She looked up. William stood in front of her with a fake smile, his hands entwined together and resting calmly in front of him.

"Fine," she said and went back to typing the report that was due in three days. The final report before this final merger was officially over and she'd have to decide whether to continue on in Italy or leave the company. "Bring her in."

"Now friend," he said with an edge in his tone. Lizzie put her pen down and looked up, annoyed. He didn't have that demure smile anymore and his hands were now on his waist. "Your tone is not giving off harmonious vibes, which is what you are supposed to be doing. Harmonious merger is your thing, it's what pays our salaries, you even copyrighted it. May I suggest you calm the hell down, have a drink, take a Valium, call the man who's making you bark at your staff . . . do something, Lizzie, because it's been over two weeks of your wrath and it's getting kinda Miranda Priestly, without the . . . ya know . . ." He waved his hand in a dismissive circle in front of her face. "The flawless designer clothes and millions of dollars. And quite frankly, I love you to death, but I'm not going to stick around and take the bullshit."

Lizzie looked down at her suit and straightened her lapels. Yes, she hadn't washed her hair in a week and makeup felt like the worst kind of torture, but she had on a nice suit. She wasn't a total mess.

Oh, who was she kidding. She was a disaster. She put her head down on her desk. "Your *Devil Wears Prada* references are duly noted. I'll tone it down." Her voice was muffled.

William came around and patted her back. "Lizzie, the way I see it, you have two choices here. You either call the man and get closure or you cut ties and move on. Moping around and yelling at everyone isn't going to do you any good. It certainly isn't doing a thing for me."

"I know. I know." She wasn't the kind of person who

second-guessed herself. "I've always been so decisive. I've never needed closure. I don't know why I just can't move on. I keep replaying that stupid kiss in my head. Did he meet her at the beach and get caught by the paparazzi? Did she seduce him and he just had a lapse in judgment? Had they been screwing the entire time right under my nose? God, William, I feel so stupid." She banged her head lightly on her desk.

William squeezed her shoulder. "This is becoming very *Groundhog Day.*" He said it because they kept having the same conversation. It was embarrassing. She'd never been the kind of woman who hyper hyper-focused on what a guy said or didn't say.

"Oh my God, who even am I?"

"Suck it up, buttercup. Maybe he did do those things or maybe it was all photoshopped—"

"Then why hasn't he called? If it was photoshopped or a misunderstanding, he would've called and said as much, right? He just let me go, he didn't even try to explain. He hasn't set the record straight online. It's as if I dreamed those four days in my head. I couldn't have been the only one who had feelings?"

They'd been through all this, back and forth, countless times over the last two weeks.

"Stop sulking. You're Lisette Alonso. You'll figure this out; just like everything you do, it'll work out. Right now, however, you need to do something about the hideous bun on your head and the smeared eyeliner so that I can tell your two o'clock to come in before your one o'clock decides to stroll in."

"Ugh . . . I hate you," she said, pulling out a mirror from her drawer.

"And I love you too." He patted her face with a tissue while she fixed her hair. "This too shall pass, Lizzie. I promise."

"What would I do without you, William?"

"I know, right?" he said with a wink.

Well, she always had Mari as a backup.

Mari took a different approach from William's.

"Remind me never to take a transatlantic cruise," Mari said a few days later when she returned from her honeymoon. "I've been out of my mind trying to get in touch with you. First of all, how are you doing? You look fabulous, by the way."

"You are a liar and I love you for that." Lizzie blew her nose into a tissue. It was late at night and Mari had finally been able to FaceTime. "How was your honeymoon?"

"Lotsa sex, great food, a lot of alcohol, yada yada yada. Typical honeymoon. But I'm not here for that, I'm here because I saw the photos."

"The entire world saw the photos. It's mortifying. I was cheated on in real time."

"Asshole Anderson, I knew it. He could not be trusted," Mari seethed. It wasn't making Lizzie feel any better. "This isn't your fault, honey. The man had us both fooled. Take some time off and grieve; once you get it all out, you'll feel better."

Mari did not give great advice, but she meant well.

"I am boycotting the Invader movie. Fuck him and his stupid books and his stupid movie. I'll never watch another Violet Gram movie either," Mari said.

"Thanks for the solidarity, Mari." She wiped her eyes. She hadn't been able to stop crying.

"Call me anytime. I'm here for you, Lizzie."

"Thanks, Mari. Love you."

Since Lizzie had returned from Mexico, she'd been bombarded with reporters on her doorstep and at work. But it had been nearly three weeks now and a new, hotter scandal had broken out somewhere, which meant that the reporters had backed off. And as life tended to do, it moved on.

The problem was that she didn't think she'd ever really get over this heartbreak. Her love had been real and she'd been more vulnerable with Brian than she'd been with any other man in her life. Jason cheating on her had been rough; Brian cheating on her and the world feeling pity for her had been brutal.

Brian

I read the outline of book ten," Louise said over the phone.

"Yeah? And what did you think?" Brian was in his garage

sanding a wooden barn door that he wanted to repurpose into a dining room table.

"I think that the shit with that Alonso girl made you stupid."

He put the sandpaper down. "What?"

"Oh, Brian, Brian, Brian. Silly male." This older woman who he'd cared about, who had helped make his career, who had supported him and entertained all his quirks began to laugh. It was the nasally laugh of someone who'd spent years smoking.

"Not funny, Lu."

"Oh, honey, it's hilarious, actually," she said. "Do you ever get tired of sitting there and just letting things happen to you? You wrote a book that happened to become a hit, which happened to land in the hands of a movie executive. You happened to be pretend engaged and you happened to accidentally kiss Violet Gram. Do you take responsibility for anything, Brian? You're a smart man, one of the smartest, actually. Yet you have no ownership of anything."

He held out his phone and looked at the screen. Had he been talking to Louise? Was this a dream?

"Hello? Did your brain explode or something?" she asked.

"Yes, actually. I think it did," he admitted. "I take ownership of things, Louise. I worked hard to write my books. I liked this last one. If you didn't enjoy it you could just say so, like you have nine times before."

"I agree that you work hard on your books," she said. "But then you don't lift a finger. Do you know how many authors work their asses off promoting their books just to sell a couple of hundred? You got lucky, my friend. One big book influencer liked it and then it snowballed."

"It's not luck. My books are good."

"How many good books do you think I see on my desk? Hundreds, Brian. Yes, the book needs to be good, and I agree you wrote phenomenal books, but there's also the luck factor and you, Brian, are so fucking lucky, I can't even quantify it."

He'd never thought of that.

"You have zero social media presence. You sit at home whittling furniture, skipping events, and your books are still selling off the shelves like hotcakes."

"You know I'll make it worse if I actually go to an event. I always say the wrong things."

"But you also don't make any efforts to fix it. You can see a therapist, a doctor, a damn hypnotherapist . . . anything. You are not the first person to get stage fright. You are not the only person that gets uncomfortable in social situations. You can make an effort of some sort, but you don't. Why?"

"Bec—"

"It was rhetorical. The answer is because you haven't needed to. And now, your face is plastered everywhere. You're a home-wrecker to some and a lucky son of a bitch to others. I warned you about Violet."

"I know! And I stayed away!"

"But you kissed her anyway."

"She kissed me!"

"Semantics, darling, semantics."

"Lizzie left. She fucking left and didn't wait for an explanation. That's not my fault."

"But it is your problem."

"How so?"

"In all the years we've been working together, I've been your biggest cheerleader. I may give you some suggestions but all in all, your books are phenomenal. This one is dog shit."

"Jesus, Louise. Don't hold back."

"Don't worry. I wasn't planning to. If I send this to your editor she'll think you've lost your mind. It's not just dog shit, it's actually cruel. Your readers have been waiting for years for the big happily-ever-after you sold them through nine books of metaphorical foreplay and you killed the hero in the book. No, wait! The heroine murdered the hero in the book. In cold blood."

"Her motive—"

"Was bullshit. You half-assed a motive. You turned a romantic dystopian masterpiece into a horror novel."

"Everyone misses the mark sometimes. I'll revise it." Perhaps he'd been a wee bit mad when he began rewrites.

"This is beyond salvageable, kid. I'm old enough to be your mother so I'm going to give you a little bit of unsolicited advice. Take ownership of your shit, Brian. She may have left you but most women want to be wooed, they want someone to fight for them. She was wrong for not hearing you out, but you didn't even try. You didn't go after her. Do you even care?"

"Do I care?" Seething in anger, he grabbed the nearest object, which happened to be a hammer, tossed it across the room, making a huge hole in the wall. At the moment, he couldn't care less. "I can't stop thinking about her. I can't sleep. I can't eat. Sometimes I feel like I can't breathe, Louise. I fucking care!" he roared. "I care, damn it. I care so much I feel paralyzed."

"Then do something about it."

"Like what?"

"I can't tell you what to do, Brian. I can only tell you that you fucked up and now you need to fix it. And meanwhile, please, for the love of God, do not write one more word because at this point, Gwinnie and Zeth are headed for a Freddy Krueger kind of ending."

Chapter Thirteen

Lizzie

It had been almost a month since Mexico. Since she'd seen Brian. It was supposed to be fake yet all she'd done was think about him and how they'd ended things. She should be over it by now.

"You okay?" William asked. "You have that faraway look again."

"I do not." She closed her laptop. She'd made a conscious decision to be fine. If she acted fine, eventually she would be fine.

Also she had made another major decision, and her brain was jumbled with too many emotions. She was not going to Italy. For the first time in her life she felt lost. Did she stay in London? Did she move back home? Where was home? She knew she wanted to open a consulting firm, but where?

"Are you crying?"

"No," she said, running the bottom of her palm up her nose. William rolled his eyes.

"Scoot over, tough-ass Alonso. It's time you moved on." He nudged her where she lay on her bed.

"I am better. I've moved on. It was fake and I'm fine. I'm about to get my period, is all."

"Fine, let's change the subject. Let's talk about next week," he said. The merger was finalized and everything was moving smoothly. She wasn't needed anymore. That was her life theme—people needed her and then they didn't. "I've packed up all your stuff but I don't know where to move it to."

"Just move it all here," she said. It was Friday afternoon and William had come by to check on her on his way out to do something fun, which is what single thirty-somethings did on Friday nights. Except she didn't really feel like it. William had decided he'd stay on an extra month with the firm and come work with Lizzie once she settled on where she'd open the business. "I'm seeing some virtual real estate in Miami, New York, Boston, and here. I'll make the decision as soon as I see what my options are."

"Remember the good ol' days when you used to be decisive?"

"I may decide to cut you off from my wine supply if you don't stop messing with me," she said playfully. He was right, though. She used to be decisive and now she was just a big mess of uncertainty.

"Fine." He put his glass down and kissed her forehead.

"I'll come by Sunday for brunch and to continue to watch you wallow in self-pity."

"Thanks, you're a doll. Lock the door behind you!" she said, then: "Who are you talking to?" she yelled from her room.

"You have a package. I signed for it."

He returned inside, inspecting a package with a grin on his face. "It's from Boston. Do you know anyone from Boston?" He tossed it at her. Her brows furrowed. There was only one person she knew in Boston and William knew that. She sat up, legs crossed, and opened the package. It was a manuscript. It wasn't titled yet but it said "B. Anderson" on it.

There was also a sticky note on the front: *Lizzie, I know you hate me right now, but you were wrong, nothing happened between Violet and me. I wish you would've let me explain. I wish I would've been less hardheaded and called. There's so many things I wish I would have done differently. I fucked it all up and now I think I may be too late. The only thing I could think of to make it right was this. Please read it. It's the final Invaders book. Love, Brian.*

William took it out of her hand. "Oh my God. This is his manuscript. I bet his own editor doesn't have it yet. You have to let me read it," he begged.

Love, Brian.

She yanked it from his hand and fanned it. "I don't know if I can do this. Why is he sending me a book?"

"I think you should read it. Afterward, you'll share it

with me." He hopped back on her bed. "Better yet, let's read it together!"

"Bye, Will," she said, pushing him off the bed. She felt as if she were holding a live grenade.

"Ugh. Bye."

Her heart was thrumming against her chest again. Now, however, it was for a different reason. Why had Brian sent her the book? What could he possibly have written in it to make any difference at all?

She hugged it to her chest, unable to pay any attention to whatever she had been watching on television a minute ago, because she had Brian's manuscript. He'd written it with his own hands. He'd touched it. She hugged it tighter.

She didn't know if she could read it. It was too painful; even if the book had nothing to do with her, with them, it came from him and that made it too difficult.

But even if she didn't know how she'd ever forgive him, she had no choice but to start reading.

Brian

*B*rian couldn't sit at home and wait. He'd sent her his last book of the series and if she hated it, or if she rejected him, he didn't know how he could write it differently or how he'd even survive. The woman was beyond stubborn. She'd ghosted him in a way that was so final and so drastic it pissed him off. Yes, her being upset was understandable. But not listening to his side of the story was just as bad.

But fuck it all to hell. He needed to see her.

IT WAS LATE at night when he arrived at her door after taking a red-eye to London. He knocked probably more forcefully than he had intended.

The door swung open. "What are you doing here?" she asked, her eyes red and puffy. He let himself inside, shutting the door behind him.

"Did you finish the book?"

"About an hour ago. I spent all night reading."

"What did you think? Did Gwinnie make the right decision?"

"I don't know!" she yelled at him, looking pained and torn. In the book, Gwinnie made a grand gesture and the couple finally got their happily-ever-after. Like reality, it hadn't come easy but the outcome was worth all the turmoil, fights, and battles they'd overcome. He'd been wrong about it: Love wasn't cheesy. It was real and raw and passionate. Just like the way he felt about Lizzie. It wasn't easy but he'd had easy. Sylvie had been easy. Easy wasn't love, easy was just settling for what's right in front of you. Effort, blood, sweat, and tears, that was real life.

"You hurt me, Brian. It wasn't fake for me, not really. I wanted it to be but it wasn't. Seeing you kiss another woman while we were together was painful. And that's a hard thing to admit but there you have it," she said as he walked farther into her house, until the backs of her knees hit the couch and she had no choice but to sit.

"It wasn't fake for me either and if you had picked up your phone or simply stayed and talked to me, I would have explained it to you. Which I'm going to do now. Like it or not."

"It doesn't matter. I forgive you. You wouldn't have done something to intentionally hurt me, I know that now."

"You're going to listen anyway," he said. He took her hands in his and knelt in front of her so that they were eye to eye. God, he wanted to kiss her almost as much as he wanted to throttle her. "Violet kissed me. I didn't kiss her. I didn't reciprocate it. I didn't even know it was happening until her lips were on mine. She set up the press to catch that photo but I actually pushed her away, which was of course cropped out of the photos. And that article about her getting a divorce, it has nothing to do with me. She's getting a divorce because her husband finally grew a pair and left her. In fact, you should know, she is being recast. She's not going to be in the second movie or in any other Invader movie."

Her mouth opened in shock. "What?"

"I told the studio I would not promote the next movies or give them any other books if Violet was cast as Gwinnie."

"You did that? That could have cost you your career, Brian. She's Hollywood's sweetheart."

"I don't care. You're more important and it was the right

thing to do. They weren't happy but I stood my ground. I didn't want someone like her representing a character that I love so much, anyway.

"But that's a secret. No one can know until the first movie is released."

"Mum's the word," she said and zipped her lip.

"Ariana Moore is taking over." Oh, wow. In his standoff with the studio he'd also demanded that they try to get Ariana Moore to take on the role. She looked a lot like Lizzie, who happened to look a lot like Gwinnie. Ariana had jumped at the chance to play the role.

"I'm so happy it worked out so well, Brian."

"I always thought I was an uncomplicated man. I thought I wanted peace and monotony. But turns out I love passion, and complicated, stubborn women. I never fought with my ex-wife. Never. You and I, we argue about everything but that fire you have, that's why I love you and it's taken me time to understand this, but I'm not boring and I'm not uncomplicated. I'm actually kinda fucked up and I have issues and I don't need nor want peace. I need someone who takes me out of my comfort zone but holds my hand and helps me on the journey. I need someone who challenges me and wants adventures sometimes and tacos and margaritas in bed other times. I want you, Lizzie. I want you not for fake and not for just now. I want you for real and for always. I love you, Lisette Alonso."

Her eyes were full of tears leaking out slowly down her

face. "Gwinnie made the right choice in finally letting Zeth love her. The book is perfect, Brian."

"Oh, thank God," he sighed.

"I'm sorry I ran away without letting you explain. It scared me how much I loved you and I thought that if you said the words—if you ended things—I would break."

"So you thought you'd do it to me before I did it to you."

"Something like that."

He wrapped his arms around her neck and kissed her senseless.

He wiped the tears from her eyes while he moved onto the sofa and lifted her so that she sat on his lap. "I don't want to do a long-distance relationship. I want to wake up with you and go to sleep next to you every day. And before you say this is moving too fast, I ran some numbers."

She chuckled while trying to wipe away her tears. "Is that so, Anderson? I didn't take you for a math whiz."

"I am," he said. She wasn't a crier and her tears made him love her even more. She didn't do vulnerable with most people, and the fact she felt something so deep for him it caused her to cry, what he assumed were happy tears, made his heart sore. "So, we've known each other for twenty-six years, so if my calculations are correct it's about damn time we start this relationship."

She laughed against his chest.

"Turns out I'm between careers at the moment. In fact, I am at a crossroads. I can renew the lease on this flat another year or maybe I can crash at someone's house while I figure out where I want to start my new consulting business."

"Well, you're in luck. Your boyfriend has space in his home for you. And you're also in luck that said boyfriend only needs a laptop to do his work. He can work anywhere." He tipped her head up to meet her eyes. "Seriously, though, move in with me. Come to Boston. Figure out what you want to do and where you want to do it. Don't worry about me. I really don't care where I live as long as I'm with you."

She wrapped her arms around his neck and peppered kisses all over his face. He knew he'd made the right decision by taking the leap of faith and writing the final book and coming to see her. She was his Lizzie, his home, and wherever she was felt like the right place to be.

"I love you, Brian Anderson. Thank you for giving Gwinnie and me a happily-ever-after."

Acknowledgments

This book caught me by surprise. I hadn't felt inspired and then the always wonderful Sarah Younger, agent extraordinaire, sent me an email out of nowhere with a great title and a fun idea from the lovely Tessa Woodward. And just like that, my imagination went wild and I got excited. I hadn't had this much fun writing a book in a long time. So, thank you, Tessa, for the inspiration, and Sarah, for the introduction. Without you both, this book would not have happened!

Alas, I can't end the acknowledgments without thanking my forever valentine. Without your support and patience, Gabriel, I couldn't have done it. Inspiration is one thing but being able to sit down and flesh out an entire book in a short amount of time takes help, and you are the glue that holds everything together while I'm in my writing cave. So thank you for being you. I love you more than Gwinnie loves Zeth and Lizzie loves Brian.

About the Author

SIDNEY HALSTON is the *USA Today* bestselling author of the Panic series, the Worth the Fight series, and the Iron-Clad Security novels. She worked as an attorney before picking up a pen at thirty years old to write something other than legal briefs. Born in Miami, Florida, to Cuban parents, she lives with her husband and her three children, in whom she's instilled a love of nature and an appreciation for the planet.